Natasha coul

But she refused t
crew member. "T ,
turning away from the body as she recalled the gunshots fired at her and the explosion at her home.

"I'm not going to let that happen to you. I promise."

The funny thing was, she believed Chris. She didn't know him, but there was something about him... something familiar, comforting, like the touch of his fingertips against her skin. Or was her scrambled brain imagining things?

Chris pulled away, and the moment was over. "I'm calling a team over. We need to mobilize as many resources as we can to get this figured out."

"Good plan." She'd delve into her hazy memories of this man another time. There were more important things to deal with right now. "We need to warn the other crew before it's too late."

The front window blew out, shattered by a bullet, and glass exploded at them.

She got the message, loud and clear: it was already too late.

Michelle Karl is an unabashed bibliophile and romantic suspense author. She lives in Canada with her husband and an assortment of critters, including a codependent cat and an opinionated parrot. When she's not reading and consuming copious amounts of coffee, she writes the stories she'd like to find in her "to be read" pile. She also loves animals, world music and eating the last piece of cheesecake.

Books by Michelle Karl

Love Inspired Suspense

Fatal Freeze
Unknown Enemy
Outside the Law
Silent Night Threat

Silent Night Threat

Michelle Karl

HARLEQUIN® LOVE INSPIRED® SUSPENSE

Recycling programs for this product may not exist in your area.

ISBN-13: 978-0-373-67862-4

Silent Night Threat

This edition published by arrangement with Love Inspired Books.

www.Harlequin.com

Printed in U.S.A.

When I consider thy heavens, the work of thy fingers,
the moon and the stars, which thou hast ordained;
What is man, that thou art mindful of him?
and the son of man, that thou visitest him?

—*Psalms* 8:3-4

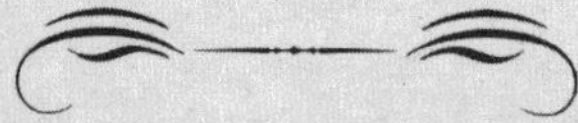

For Dave, Micah and Dad, who get the joke.

ONE

The nameplate on the gold bracelet that circled her wrist read *Natasha.* She winced at the sharp pain that split the back of her skull as she moved into a seated position and twisted the shiny chain, searching for something—anything—that might provide a clue as to what she was doing lying by the side of the road with a gun in her hand.

A gun! She scrambled backward in the dirt, leaving the weapon behind. A rumble in the distance told her a car was headed her way. Should she leave the gun there or throw it into the ditch?

Where am I? It felt as though her entire head was on fire, and black spots clouded her vision when she turned to try to take in her surroundings. What little she could make out didn't help: a long road, grass on either side, trees along the edge of the grass. She sniffed the air but didn't smell anything beyond lingering exhaust fumes, dirt and copper. *Copper?*

Warmth blossomed along the right side of her temple, a thicker and more concentrated heat than the sun's rays beating down overhead during this unusually warm afternoon. Where was she? What day was it? What month, for that matter? No one with any sense would be lying outside midday in the heat and humidity, regardless of the location or time of year. She lifted her hand to the side of her head and touched something hot and sticky. Alarm shot through her insides as her fingers pulled back, slick with deep, crimson blood.

It's not bright red, she thought. *I've been here for a little while, at least.*

But she had no idea how she'd gotten there. Or why. Or if she should even trust the bracelet around her wrist. *Natasha?* It sounded vaguely familiar, but felt strange as she rolled the word around on her tongue. She needed to get back to the city and ask… *Ask who? What city?*

Panic rose as her brain refused to recall important details. How did she get here? Did anyone know where she was, and would anyone miss her? Where did she work? Where did she live?

Her breath grew shallow as the lack of details increased in scope, and while some part of her cerebral cortex recognized the danger in hyperventilating while already injured and lying out in the sun, she couldn't quell the sense of terror that threatened to send her consciousness retreating back into darkness. The black spots in her vision grew larger as the roar of the engine grew louder.

I should move, she thought, but her limbs refused to budge. *I should get out of here, away from the gun. What if I've done something terrible?*

A large shape passed by, and the vehicle engine cut out. The shape came into focus between the black spots at the same time as she heard a car door open and footsteps crunch across the side of the road toward her.

"Ma'am? Are you all right?"

She couldn't respond. She didn't know how, and her voice refused to cooperate. The person became clearer as he moved closer—a man with dark hair and a tanned complexion, bearing the broad shoulders of a weight lifter. She knew that because she lifted weights, too.

She did? She did!

I remember that, at least.

"I'm Special Agent Chris Barton of the FBI,

and I'm here to help." The man crouched, entering her field of vision. "Looks like you could use a ride to the hospital." His gaze flicked down, concern blossoming across his features. She followed his line of sight, confused…and then remembered a gun sat only a few feet away from her. "Hang on… Natasha? Natasha Stark?"

"I—I don't know."

"You don't know what?"

"Who that is."

His eyes widened and cut sideways, toward the gun. Her stomach lurched as his hand slipped inside his pocket. Was he going to arrest her? "And that's not mine. I think."

"You think?"

"I don't know." She pressed the heels of her hands against her temples, trying to quell the throbbing, but the motion only sent a fresh wave of ache through whatever wounds marked her head and face. "I'm not sure. I don't remember. I can't remember anything." She looked up at him and stilled a gasp of surprise at the sudden wave of familiarity that washed over her. She couldn't place him, but she didn't automatically flinch as he reached for her, brushing his fingers across the top of her head.

A hiss escaped from between his teeth, and she pulled away in alarm.

"Sorry," he said, inching closer in his crouch. "You've got a nasty gash and growing goose eggs on different parts of your head. When you say you can't remember anything, what do you mean? Your name? Where you are? How you got here? Who *I* am?"

She shrugged, her eyes becoming hot with tears. She blinked them away—this was no time to let emotions take over.

She couldn't remember, and everything hurt. "All of the above. I mean that I can't remember *anything*."

"Nothing at all? You're sure you don't recognize me?"

She tried to shake her head, but the motion caused a spark of pain to rocket through her temple. She sucked air through her teeth instead of offering a response. What had he called her? Natasha? *Like the bracelet*, she thought. *My name. It must be my name.*

"Okay, okay. That's not ideal. Look, I'm going to make a call and get an ambulance and the local police down here," he said. "It's going to be all right, but I don't want to hurt you further." He pursed his lips as he looked at her, brow furrowed.

Natasha couldn't help but stare at his arms, flexed and tense as he rested them on his knees as he crouched. Well-defined muscles stood out in all the right places, and his dark brown eyes shone with kindness and concern. "What is it? Should I recognize you? Have we met?"

"It's okay if you don't remember right now. Don't exert yourself—we can discuss it later. Hang on a sec." He stood and ran back to his blobby vehicle—her vision still hadn't cleared up enough to make out a proper shape—and returned with a water bottle and holding a dark blue shirt sporting the bright yellow letters *FBI*. He uncapped the bottle and poured a splash of water on it. "This should help. It's a little cold, but that will probably feel good. You've got a lot of blood and dirt on your face. You can use the shirt to wipe it off if you want, but you might also need this to stanch any bleeding that starts up again."

"Is that likely?"

"I have no idea. I'm an FBI agent, not a doctor."

What did she have to lose? She ran the garment across her face. The water was chilly and refreshing, which momentarily diverted her attention from the pain that kept leaping from one side of her skull to the other. She rubbed the shirt gently across her forehead and back, wincing as the fabric came in contact with the place where she'd drawn back sticky fingers minutes earlier.

"Let me help," he said, reaching for the shirt as she pulled it away from her face. "I can turn it inside out and pour a little more water on it."

She'd looked up at him as he moved forward to take the garment, now grimy with dirt and blood, but he remained still as a statue in his half crouch, mouth open and fingers brushing the edge of the material. He blinked rapidly, all color drained from his cheeks as he stared at her wrist. Her bracelet? She touched it, then glanced up to meet his eyes.

"I'm Natasha," she said. "But you said something else. My last name."

He nodded, gaze flicking back to the shiny bracelet. "Stark. Your name is Natasha Stark, you're an astronaut with NASA's Orion space program, and twenty-four hours ago, you disappeared."

Christopher Barton hardly believed his eyes. It was nearly impossible to reconcile the woman sitting in the dirt with the memory of the last time he'd seen her. Twelve years ago, Natasha Stark had been a shrinking image in his rearview mirror as he'd driven away from her and the future they'd planned on having together, and for those twelve years he'd done everything he could to put the memory of his first and only love out of his mind.

And now here she was, tossed right back into it. All it had taken was joining the FBI and getting reassigned to Brevard County in Florida after his two-year probation as a new agent, combined with raising his hand on a missing person's case that had come up early this morning. He should have asked who the missing person was before volunteering to spearhead the search. He should have also backed down the moment he realized that it was none other than Natasha Stark, his former fiancée.

He could still scarcely believe it, and yet here she was, sitting on the ground with a gun by her side, looking up at him as though she'd never seen him before in her life. Something was very, very wrong.

"Natasha... Stark?" she asked, voice wavering. He took the shirt from her outstretched hand, and sunlight glinted off the gold bracelet around her wrist. His breath caught, and he didn't trust himself to say another word. "I believe you. Good thing I wore my bracelet," she mumbled, and he wasn't sure if she was being serious or trying to make a joke. "I'm fortunate you recognized me with a face this dirty. Or did the bracelet help with that, too?"

"It didn't have to," he said, willing his limbs to move. He poured more water on the shirt and pressed it against her head as gently as possible. His entire body had begun to tremble, and his ankles wobbled in the crouch. He'd thought he'd be fine, once he found her. That it wouldn't matter. Twelve years was a long time. "Hold this here. Looks like you're not bleeding anymore, but just in case."

"What do you mean it didn't have to?"

Was she playing with him? It would be just like Natasha to play a prank on him—like the Natasha he knew twelve years ago, when they were still kids. Well, technically not kids but teenagers, but it seemed like more than a lifetime ago. The way she looked at him now, though...he didn't see any mirth. She looked nervous and scared.

He tried to put the pieces together. Head trauma, confusion and a gun within reach. According to NASA, she hadn't shown up for an appointment yesterday morning and no one had been able to get in touch with her since, putting the timeline since she'd been missing at approximately twenty-four hours. He'd only searched this area of highway based on a tip a passerby had phoned in to local police. This wasn't the kind of case the FBI would normally be called in on, but Natasha's situation wasn't normal. He'd never in a million years have anticipated that she would become, of all things, an astronaut. It meant working with other people from different walks of life, different economic backgrounds, in a more sensitive capacity than many other jobs. International partnerships were on the line, and occasionally crew members on the same team didn't even speak the same language or more than a few common critical words and phrases. Not exactly the kind of thing her parents had been great at, and he'd thought their influence had rubbed off on her. They might still be together if it hadn't.

He pulled his phone out of his pocket and tapped it against the palm of his hand. "Let's try to put some pieces together while we wait for help to arrive. What's the last thing you can remember?"

A shallow sigh escaped her lips. "I'm not sure. But what you said sounds right…feels right. NASA? Yeah. I think I went in for…a physical exam. No, I was on my way to a physical exam. A checkup."

"That's a good start. You're doing great. Can you tell me anything about that appointment? What time? What building?" She started to shake her head but grimaced at the movement. A humming in the distance cut through the sounds of nature and the occasional whoosh of a passing car, but he focused his attention on Natasha. She definitely needed a doctor and fast. Head trauma wasn't the kind of injury that a person could take their time getting checked out, and considering the important details she'd already forgotten… Well, the longer the delay, the more severe the injury could become. Right now, she didn't even remember herself, let alone *him*.

"At work," she mumbled. "Because I was in space."

"Even better. See? You haven't forgotten everything." He tried to reassure her and keep her calm as the buzzing noise grew louder. Were they near an airfield? He didn't think so. "Sit tight. An ambulance will be here soon. A lot of people have been looking for you, and they'll be glad to hear you're all right."

"Thank you." Her gaze shifted past his shoulder. She squinted, like she couldn't figure out what she saw. "Is that a drone?"

Chris twisted to look as a sudden gust of air

whipped past his cheek. Dirt kicked up in the small space between them.

She coughed. “What was that?”

“That’s definitely a drone,” he said, taking in the boxy shape and the rotating blades that whipped around at high speeds to keep the device aloft. “What is it doing out here?”

The drone dropped several feet and moved closer—and this time, Chris heard the muffled bang.

“It’s shooting at us!” Natasha shouted, dropping the borrowed T-shirt. Alarm flared in Chris’s stomach. He lunged for her and wrapped her in his arms, picked her up and then dived for cover behind his truck as the drone released another shot. He opened the passenger door and lifted Natasha inside. They couldn’t stay out in the open; the drone operator could maneuver around to the other side of the vehicle and easily continue shooting.

“Lie down in there,” he instructed. “Make yourself into as small a target as possible. Cover your head.” She did as he instructed, and as soon as she was in position, Chris climbed in on her side, stepping over her to slide into the driver’s seat. A bullet slammed against his door with a clank as he started the Suburban. His window cracked and bowed inward, protecting them for now, but the bulletproof glass could only take so many hits. Without hesitation, he stepped on the gas and veered his SUV back onto the road, heart pounding in his chest.

"Tasha? You still with me?" His insides tightened as he anticipated her response.

"Yes" came her thin, choked reply. "Is it gone?"

He checked the rearview mirror. The drone still hovered in the air, but it didn't appear to be following them. He continued checking as they drove away, and eventually the machine became a black dot in the distance. Who on earth would use a drone to shoot at Natasha? He supposed it was possible that the drone had been shooting at him, but an armed drone was the kind of weapon to be used on a fixed target—it took time to fly one, and the operator needed to know where to go. He'd been driving around for hours. She'd been by the side of the road for who knew how long. It seemed like an inefficient and cumbersome way to assassinate a person, even though it did provide an element of anonymity. Unless the police were able to take the thing down. He hadn't gotten a good look at it, but a weaponized drone was no small thing to buy, equip and maneuver with accuracy. And if someone wanted to kill her outright, why on earth had he found Natasha lying in the dirt with no memory of how she'd gotten there and with a gun by her side?

"It's gone," he said. "Do you have any idea why someone would be shooting at you?"

She grew silent. Her shuddery breathing told him that not only was she in physical pain but the situation had already begun to take a mental toll. He had no doubt that once she got cleaned up and received treatment for her injuries, she'd be much better equipped to begin dealing with what was clearly memory loss.

"I'm going to use my radio to contact local police and let them know what happened here—all right? When I went to get water for you earlier, I let the FBI know I'd found you, and they contacted emergency services." She responded with a barely audible affirmative as he fired up his Bluetooth system to make the call. "But now that we're in the car, I'd rather not wait. We should get you to a hospital to get looked over."

As he called in the incident to police dispatch, Natasha worked her way back up to a seated position and buckled in. From the corner of his eye, he could see she appeared to be struggling to remain conscious. He needed to get her to a doctor as quickly as possible.

"Try to stay awake," he said. "I know it's hard and you must be in a lot of pain, but it's going to be a whole lot worse if you fall asleep. I'll get you into good hands as fast as I can, so just—"

Bam! His vehicle swerved to the right before he reacted to the hit. The Suburban's tires crunched against dirt as he gripped the wheel and corrected the vehicle's course.

What in the world...? He checked the rearview mirror and saw nothing, then turned his head just as a second hit slammed against them, once again slightly bumping the SUV off course. With his head turned, Chris saw a navy blue Range Rover with deeply tinted windows hiding in his blind spot. He couldn't see the driver through the front windshield, but he had a bad feeling about the situation.

After all, *someone* had to have been in charge of the drone. And it appeared that they weren't pleased that Chris had found Natasha. There was no doubt in his mind—someone wanted to kill Tasha Stark, and he'd just become her human shield.

TWO

Natasha braced against the door and seat. Another slam against the side of the vehicle attempted to push them off the road, but the man who'd rescued her—*Chris? Yes, Chris*—had a firm grip on the wheel and kept them on course. His biceps and forearms flexed from the strain of each hit, and his jaw was set in a determined grimace. She blinked against the exhaustion that had started to call to her, telling her to close her eyes and surrender to the darkness. But Chris's earlier words and a memory deep within her consciousness told her that she had to remain awake at all costs.

She strained to look over the back of the seat and out the rear window, despite the agony of turning her head. The blue Range Rover had dropped back, moving away from the side of their vehicle.

"Are they done?" she mumbled. "Will they

leave us alone, since they clearly aren't going to get us off the road that way?"

Chris shook his head and spoke through clenched teeth. "There's more than one way to run a car off the road."

"It looks like they're done, though. They're slowing down."

She wasn't sure if she heard correctly or if Chris actually growled under his breath. "Sit back in your seat, Tasha. Brace yourself. Please."

"But why?" She looked at him in confusion. "They're not—" She swung her gaze back at the Range Rover. Despite having dropped back moments earlier, it was now gaining on their SUV at an alarming rate. With a gasp, she sat back and tensed her shoulders just as a heavy slam against the back door sent their vehicle lurching forward. Metal scraped against metal, sending a high-pitched screech through the cabin.

"That's why," he said. He grabbed the gearshift, and their vehicle's engine revved higher, sending them lurching and then zooming forward. "Why aren't there any police around when you need them?"

"You already called them—aren't they on their way?"

"I sure hope so. I'd call again if I didn't need all my focus to make sure we stay on the road." As if on cue, the truck heaved again, but this time a sickening crunch accompanied the hit. Another hit followed only a few seconds afterward, and the SUV swayed from side to side. In the mirror, she saw a piece of metal go flying from their vehicle into the ditch. *The license plate!*

Please, Lord. Help us. Natasha swallowed down her fear as a sense of peace and assurance settled across her shoulders. *I haven't forgotten You. I know You're here.*

Despite the direness of the situation, she had a strong faith—that much she remembered. God was with her, even in times like this. She didn't need to panic.

"Tell me how to use your radio system," she said, taking deep breaths to manage the rolling waves of ache in her head that seemed to increase with every jolt of the vehicle. "I'll tell the police which direction we're headed in case they're coming from the other way."

"Are you sure?" Chris poked at a button. The next slam against the SUV caused them to swerve since he had only one hand on the wheel.

"You need to keep us on the road," she said.

"We need help, and I don't know how else to get it."

"All right." His gaze flicked over to take her in, probably to make sure she was conscious enough to handle it. "There's a button on the right that says—"

He'd looked at her for a fraction of a second, maybe less, but it was enough.

The next hit clipped the SUV in just the right way. The wheels slipped against the asphalt, and they skidded across the roadside stretch of dirt, tipping them toward the ditch. Their vehicle bucked, leaned and tilted sideways. Natasha screamed as they went airborne, the remnants of a prayer on her lips as Chris's strong arms reached out to grab her and pull her toward him, away from the window.

The SUV landed on its side in the ditch, and she and Chris jerked sideways in their restraints. As the airbags exploded, slamming their heads back against the headrests, Natasha tasted blood in her mouth, and her vision was once again nothing but sparks. She tried to speak, but no words came as she struggled for breath. Something hissed, and the creak of metal under tension echoed in her ears before the world grew deathly silent.

She didn't hear anything. Nothing at all, and that seemed even more frightening than before.

Her blood ran cold as a car door slammed.

As the world came back into sound and focus, Chris heard the wail of sirens growing rapidly louder. Somewhere nearby, a car door slammed. The crunch of tires against pavement told him that a vehicle had just driven away. He dared to hope that it meant the Range Rover was not only done with them but in the police's sights.

He flailed his free arm, searching for Natasha, and a momentary surge of panic took hold as he realized that he couldn't hear her breathing. Then she released a long sigh, and relief flooded through his every pore. She was still alive. But if she did indeed have a concussion, all of those hits would have made it exponentially worse. She needed to get to a hospital without further delay—they'd be able to call the right people to come and take care of her and close off his involvement in her life. If the FBI didn't ask him to continue the investigation into why she'd disappeared, that was.

He didn't want to be around when she remembered him. She'd probably be angry enough as soon as she realized that her ex-fiancé had put his arms around her, even to save her life. As soon as Natasha was secure at the hospital and the officer in charge at his FBI branch gave him the go-ahead, he'd be on his way and out of her life again, just like she'd wanted twelve years ago.

Despite having tried so hard to forget, the memory came too easily. He had been eighteen years old; she'd been seventeen. She'd worn a yellow sundress with tiny white flowers, the hem of the dress swishing above her knees, despite the cooler temperatures of late November. Her auburn hair had been knotted above her head in a messy bun, with loose strands falling about her face and framing her sharp features. Around her neck had been a topaz gemstone set among three diamonds, a beautiful piece of jewelry given to her on her sixteenth birthday by her father. It had looked completely out of place on a girl who stood barefoot in the sunshine with a wrist full of plastic bead bracelets. Under those plastic beads, he'd hoped, was the gold name bracelet he'd given her as a promise six months before proposing. But he hadn't been able to see it, and for some reason that had hurt almost as much as the small diamond ring that her father had yanked out of her hand and practically thrown at him when Chris refused to take it from Natasha's open palm. *Go*, the man had said. *She's done with you. Don't bother our family with your filth again. She's too good for you, and you know it. Come here again, and I'll have you arrested.*

Chris had looked past the man's shoulder, his eyes pleading, his heart aching with painful disbelief. Natasha had wrapped her arms around her middle, protective and closed off to him. She'd understood his unspoken question, but had only narrowed her eyes and shaken her head.

That simple gesture had said it all. And when she'd opened her mouth as if to speak to him, to explain, he didn't want to hear it. He'd turned around and left—the city, the state, the entire South—to try to banish the pain of her rejection. What had ever made him think that someone like Natasha could truly love him? She'd been a rich, spoiled girl with a daddy who handed everything to her on a silver platter—including his prejudiced beliefs. Chris should've known that they'd surface in her eventually. He should've known she wouldn't think he was good enough for her. Just because his family lived in low-income housing. Just because they relied on food stamps and welfare. He couldn't afford to get arrested, for Natasha's father to follow through on his threat. His family couldn't afford it; they needed Chris's meager paycheck to get by. No, he couldn't buy Natasha pretty things, but even with helping his family out, he'd worked odd jobs and saved for more than a year to buy her a diamond ring, like she deserved.

Sure, they were young, but he'd thought their love was stronger than that.

If she hated him so much, if she'd thought she was so much better than him, why had she even given him the time of day in the first place?

"Sir? Can you hear me?" The authoritative voice of a police officer cut through the painful memories. Chris had worked hard to turn his family's situation around. They still struggled, but since joining the FBI, he'd been able to move his parents to a decent home that they could finally call their own. He'd bought a used car for his little brother last month, so he could have an easier time making ends meet and staying out of jail. Money and status weren't what mattered for his family, and they never had been. He couldn't say the same of the Starks. The arrest of Natasha's uncle a few months ago—the former vice chairman of the Joint Chiefs of Staff at the Pentagon—had made that clearer than ever.

Maybe it was a blessing that Natasha hadn't recognized him right away.

"There are two of us in the cab," Chris called back to the officer. "An agent of the FBI and a woman who's seriously injured and needs immediate medical assistance."

"Emergency services are on their way," the officer said. "Hold tight."

That was exactly what Chris planned to do—despite how much it hurt.

Natasha balked at the doctor as he delivered the news. Even his cheerful, Christmas-light-patterned bow tie didn't help ease the shock. Psychogenic and retrograde amnesia, he told her.

Amnesia, really? She felt much better with the pain medication in her system, and the doctors had even confirmed that despite the bumps and cuts on her head, she hadn't physically sustained anything more than a mild concussion, whiplash and various cuts and bruises. She could hardly take it all in as the doctor suggested that whatever had happened to her before Special Agent Barton found her had been severe and shocking. Her initial head trauma had likely caused the retrograde amnesia, but more disturbing was the suggestion that her autobiographical memory loss had been caused by intense psychological stress.

"We can definitely confirm that you are Natasha Stark," said the doctor. *Dr. Olsen*, she read off his name tag. "We've printed out this info sheet for you with your name, address and medical history. I recommend you keep this with you on your person for the time being, in case any additional medical issues arise. That said, you're probably going to want to head over to Titusville as soon as possible so they can have a look at you."

Natasha blinked at the sheet a nurse handed her. This was her, her identity, all on an eight-and-a-half-by-eleven-inch piece of paper. The name and address evoked a strong feeling of home, but she couldn't picture it. She closed her eyes, trying to remember. It didn't work.

"When will I get my memories back?" She attempted to hide the hitch in her voice. "And why would I go to Titusville? I see that I live there, but what do you mean? Who wants to look at me?"

Dr. Olsen looked over his shoulder at someone in the back of the room, then back at her. "Agent Barton says you work at NASA. That,

I'm happy to say, is absolutely true. You were due to report at Kennedy Space Center yesterday for one of your scheduled checkups."

"You said as much to me yourself when I found you." Chris emerged from behind the doctor, a limp magazine in his hand. "Only you never arrived for the physical. And since NASA is a government agency, we were called when you didn't report as scheduled."

Dr. Olsen chuckled and smiled at Natasha. She liked him; he seemed kind. "Three weeks ago, Ms. Stark, you were looking at this planet from space. You just returned from a six-month mission in low-Earth orbit on the Orion, testing that new Deep Space Module everyone's been talking about. Well, everyone in the scientific community, that is. Based on the success of your mission, looks like NASA's really pulled ahead with their plans to launch the first manned mission to Mars."

"How do you know that?" Chris asked. "That can't be in her medical records."

Dr. Olsen smiled sheepishly. "No, but I do have a niece in her daughter's class at school. Hayley must be happy to have you back, Ms. Stark."

"Daughter?" She had a daughter! Why couldn't she remember her own child? She felt even more desperate to get her memories back. The face of a girl with curly chestnut locks and expressive eyes materialized in her mind like a developing Polaroid—young, preteen, with an affinity for sparkly pink lip gloss and purple chokers.

"Daughter?" Chris echoed. "How old is she?"

"How old is Hayley?" Dr. Olsen tapped a pen against his clipboard. "My niece is in sixth grade, so that'd put the students around eleven or twelve years old, I'd think."

"Twelve years old," Chris murmured. "I see."

Natasha's mental image solidified, carrying a wave of emotions, smells and sensations. The comfort of a soft, fragile baby as it lay in her arms. The stern face of an older man—her father?—as he entered the room. This caused a sudden rush of fear that shifted the scene into a new memory of standing in the middle of a department store, arms laden with a heavy basket of shampoo, a pair of child's sneakers and laundry soap, as her head whipped from one side to the other, searching. *"Hayley, honey?"* she'd called, heart beating faster with each passing second. *"Sweetheart, where are you? Hayley?"* Relief had flooded her veins as a cherub-cheeked toddler burst out from under a clothing rack, shouting, *"Surprise, Mommy!"* with arms stretched over her head in a V—and immediately, the memory shifted again and Hayley stood in the same pose, arms lifted, standing on a three-tiered podium. A gold medal gleamed around her neck, and she waved at Natasha in the crowd. She recalled feeling a swell of pride as her daughter won first place in a Florida Gold Coast special event for swimmers aged twelve and under.

Natasha exhaled slowly, concentrating on the memories of her daughter and trying to burn them into her brain. "Yes, that's correct," she said. "She turned twelve a few months ago."

Chris cleared his throat. "Does Natasha have an emergency contact listed in her file? Husband? He might be able to bring her daughter over and help jog some more memories."

Dr. Olsen scanned the chart. "There are two emergency contacts here. One is listed as a parent, not a spouse. The other is her NASA physician."

In a flash Natasha knew that was correct—and that she didn't want to talk about her parents. A glance down at her left hand confirmed what she suspected even without remembering it specifically. "I'm not married. Please don't tell me someone called my father."

The nurse in the room placed a hand on Natasha's shoulder. "Yes, dear, but I'm afraid no one was able to reach him. We tried the second emergency number for the specialized NASA physician and got through. We've been instructed to have you contact him as soon as you're able."

A knock on the door brought a second nurse into the room. "Dr. Olsen? There are officers here who'd like to take the patient's statement, now that she's stable."

"Police?" She glanced at Chris. "Why do I need to talk to the police if you're FBI?"

He held up his phone. "My job is to find you and, as of thirty minutes ago, continue to investigate your disappearance. The local authorities will go after the guy who ran us off the road and help figure out where that gun came from. We'll be working together but best to bring them up to speed on an event like this with a direct statement so they can be on the lookout."

Natasha wrapped her arms around her middle as the police officers shuffled into the room and made the appropriate introductions. One of the nurses raised the front half of the hospital bed so Natasha could speak to the officers without physical strain, which she appreciated—she already felt mentally exhausted, like her brain was attempting memory gymnastics but kept missing the landing mat. She told Officers Kirby and Lee about waking up by the side of the road with a gun in her hand, and Dr. Olsen confirmed the relevant medical details regarding her memory loss. She recounted her and Chris's harrowing escape from the drone and provided what details she could about the vehicle that had knocked them off the road.

"And you have no idea why anyone would try to kill you?" Officer Kirby looked unconvinced, his eyebrows high enough that they were almost hidden under his cap. "No known enemies?"

"I'm a scientist," she said, pinching the bridge of her nose. "An astronaut. I've never considered myself a high-value assassination target."

"You should," Chris interjected. "You're a highly trained specialist working toward national interests."

Officer Kirby cleared his throat, seemingly unappreciative of Chris's commentary. "And how did you come to have a firearm in your possession?"

"I already told you I don't know. I don't remember. I'm not a gun owner."

"So you *do* remember things about yourself."

"I don't—" A sharp pain tore through her head, and she lay back, closing her eyes. She remembered some things and not others, and she had no idea why or how. She heard Dr. Olsen tapping his pen against his clipboard again.

"I think that's enough questions for today," the doctor said, his tone stern. "Miss Stark requires rest. Her brain should recover all the missing information eventually, but you'll do neither yourselves nor your investigation any good if you push for details that she's presently unable to access."

Officer Lee pulled a card from her pocket and handed it to Natasha, then handed a second card to Chris. Natasha took hers and ran her fingers along the edges. "Call us as soon as you remember anything," the officer said with a tight but genuine smile.

"Wait," Natasha said as the officers made to exit the room. They paused. "The gun. Did you find it?" Kirby and Lee exchanged a look that caused Natasha's stomach to flip-flop.

"Yes," Officer Lee finally said. "And there's one round missing from the chamber. Your clothes have been claimed by law enforcement and are being tested for gunshot residue."

"Her clothes?" Chris stepped to Natasha's side and placed his hand on the edge of the hospital bed as if trying to protect her from the officer's words. "Why? We're the ones who were used as target practice."

"So you've said," Officer Kirby chimed in, pushing past his partner. "But it was your job to find her, yes? You've found her. Investigate why she went missing if you have to, but don't question how we choose to pursue our own investigations related to the incident. We have a firearm that's been discharged, a woman with no memory and no additional witnesses to this reported drone attack. Ms. Stark claims to have nothing to do with the firearm, and this way we can make sure of that. Wouldn't you prefer to know for certain that the gun isn't yours, Ms. Stark?"

Of course she wanted to know that for certain, but she also had a bad feeling that if the tests proved otherwise, she'd be in a world of trouble. "What happens if you find residue on my clothes?"

Officer Kirby scowled and began to speak, but Officer Lee cut in first. "It will be inconclusive," she said. "It only means the weapon was discharged within a few feet of you, not that you fired it yourself. Either way, maybe it will help put some pieces together in your own mind."

"The FBI will be pursuing the threat against Ms. Stark, specifically looking into the tech that took shots at us," Chris added. "How far will your own investigation go?"

Officer Lee shrugged. "We'll try to reconstruct the accident, wait for what the tests say and put out a BOLO for the vehicle you described, but that's really all we can do at present. My captain has ordered us to cooperate with the FBI, so we won't step on your toes on purpose." She nodded at Natasha. "I hope you get your memories back and feel better in time for Christmas, Ms. Stark. My son loves spaceships and also wants to be an astronaut when he grows up. Our entire family watched the live stream when the Orion returned."

Warmth blossomed in Natasha's cheeks as the officer smiled at her, and she wished she could remember more about the event Officer Lee described. "Thank you so much."

As the nurse ushered the officers out of the room, Chris sighed and tented his fingers, pressing them against his mouth. Something inside Natasha wanted to reach out and offer comfort, even though she had no idea why she'd want to comfort him, a complete stranger. No matter how appealing she found him. Now that she had a moment to look at him without being in the midst of panic, she had to consciously keep her mouth from falling open. He had olive skin and deep brown eyes, a square jaw and full, bow-shaped lips that she couldn't help but envy. His nearly black hair was cut short enough to not require serious maintenance but long enough to make the messy bed-head style he wore look natural. Her eyes followed the curve of his profile as he stared after the retreating forms of the police officers. His presence felt so familiar, but when she tried to rack her brain for memories, all she got in return was a fuzzy, dull ache. He seemed to sense her watching him and turned to regard her with a questioning glance. Her heart jumped as if he'd defibrillated it.

She couldn't help it. She needed to know. "How do we know each other?"

His complexion paled. "Excuse me?"

"You asked me if I recognized you, after you found me. I feel like I know you, but obviously..."

"You can't remember." He dropped his hands and shoved them in his pockets. His shoulders rose, and he stared at the floor as if trying to come up with an answer. "Natasha, the thing is—"

"Sorry, I need to interrupt for a moment." Dr. Olsen pulled several sheets of paper from his clipboard and handed them to Natasha. "These are prescriptions for painkillers and a list of recommendations as we discussed earlier in regard to managing your injuries. Please take them to your physician at NASA. Will they be arranging transportation, or will you be making your way over on your own? As long as you go there directly, I'll consent to your release."

More doctors, more tests, more paper hospital gowns? She didn't like it, but the more people with ideas about getting her memory back, the better. "Can someone call them for me?"

"We can't—"

"I'll call," said Chris. "She's my responsibility. I'll make sure she gets there safely."

She smiled at him in gratitude, but after what they'd both gone through, she also couldn't help but wonder whether going anywhere with him was safe—after all, no one had been shooting at her before this supposed FBI agent had come to her rescue.

THREE

Natasha had a twelve-year-old daughter. His relationship with Natasha Stark had ended a little over twelve years ago.

Every time he caught a glimpse of her out of the corner of his eye as they drove, he had to swallow down the lump that formed in his throat. They had been young and foolish and had made the mistake of becoming intimate before truly understanding the consequences. But even so, Chris had loved her with his whole heart. They'd stopped their covert trysts after attending a church youth rally, where Natasha had gone up to the front of the auditorium during an altar call to dedicate herself to living for Jesus and pursuing a life of faith. He hadn't been fully convinced, but he'd respected her decision and tried to do right by her. He'd talked to the leaders in her church, read his grandmother's Bible and decided that the right thing to do was propose.

Even at the time, he'd wondered if Natasha had taken to her faith so suddenly because her family demanded it of her or because she really believed. As a state senator, her father had an image to maintain, a certain theoretical family standard to uphold in order to be better positioned for reelection. Her father had never approved of him, but he hadn't interfered in their relationship. Chris had thought that asking Natasha to marry him would be enough to keep them together. Clearly he'd never been enough for *her*, either.

She was too much like her father. He hadn't wanted to believe it, but what choice had he had? She hadn't fought back or disagreed. Her father's threat ensured that he left and never contacted them again, and Chris hadn't been about to humiliate himself by groveling. And he hadn't wanted to. He'd heard what Mr. Stark called his parents when he thought Chris couldn't hear, and it wasn't a description Chris would ever repeat in polite company.

When an email had come from her, he'd deleted it. When a letter arrived, he'd burned it. If her faith and her father had turned her against him, made her believe she was better than him, he wanted nothing to do with it or with her, ever again.

And now Natasha was in his FBI vehicle, wearing clothes from the hospital lost-and-found box—a button-down plaid shirt and a pair of oversize swim trunks tied tightly at the waist. Her clothes had been taken for testing. *A twelve-year-old daughter*, he repeated to himself. *Could Natasha have kept something like that from me all this time?*

She wouldn't be able to answer that question until she got her memories back. He tried not to care, and he tried to tell himself he could be patient. Now that he worked in the area, he could ask her about Hayley someday in the future. But something deep inside persisted in wanting to be near the girl now, or at the very least catch a glimpse of Hayley. *At least then I'll know*, he thought. *One way or the other.* A father would recognize his own daughter, wouldn't he? For both their sakes, he hoped his suspicions were wrong. Then he could put it out of his thoughts and concentrate fully on wrapping up this case and getting out of Natasha's life as quickly as possible.

"Do you think we could swing by my place first?" She held the sheet from the doctor out in front of her. "It can't be too far of a detour."

Chris's heart skipped a beat. "I don't see why not. The NASA physician isn't expecting you at a certain time?"

"I'm supposed to get there as soon as possible, but there's not a set time, no. Before everyone goes home for the day, I assume." She chuckled softly, then sighed. "I'm already at an embarrassing disadvantage by not being able to remember critical pieces of information. I'd rather not further embarrass myself by showing up to my place of employment in lost-and-found couture."

"Point taken. Your address is on the sheet from the hospital, right? Punch it into the GPS, and we'll make the stop."

He turned the volume up on the radio once she'd entered the address, and the cheerful sound of Christmas carols resonated through the SUV's interior, discouraging further conversation. What would they say to each other, anyway? Any conversation would be one-sided and risk mentally taxing Natasha further. The whole situation seemed like a terrible mess, and in his professional opinion, it seemed like she'd been in the wrong place at the wrong time. A mugging gone sideways, maybe—though that didn't explain the drone or the car wreck. That was targeting, plain and simple, possibly by muggers who thought she'd caught a glimpse of their faces? It seemed a little extreme to go to such lengths, but he couldn't discount any possibility.

"It's going to be a pain replacing my ID," she muttered. "It's not like I can call the credit-card companies and confirm my identity to replace the cards. And at Christmas, too! There's no time to get this figured out and get all my cards replaced in just a week. I hope I've already done the shopping for Hayley's gifts. No child should wake up to an empty space beneath the tree. Oh, I hope I already have a tree, too."

"Maybe the credit-card company's security questions will jog your memory, or maybe those will be some of the details you didn't lose," he suggested. "You never know until you try."

"Good point." She sighed again. "And thank you. For doing this, for driving me. You didn't need to."

"I kind of did. It's been my assignment to find you, but that doesn't mean I'm going to leave you to fend for yourself after all that's happened. Besides, you haven't quite found all of yourself yet, so to speak."

She laughed, a strong, deep sound that

warmed him from the inside. He'd forgotten how much he missed that sound—and he hadn't counted on how much it would hurt to hear it again.

"I appreciate that. And I definitely could use a friendly face for a while longer. Technically, right now you're my oldest friend." She grew quiet for a few minutes before continuing the conversation. "Are you married, Agent Barton?"

"Christopher. Call me Chris."

"Okay, Chris. Are you married? Kids?"

There was that lump in his throat again. "No, can't say that I am." He sneaked a look at her. She blinked at him with her wide-eyed innocence, and it took all his restraint not to blurt out the truth. But what good would it do? Her head had started pounding at the hospital after a few questions from the police. Tossing out information from a bad situation that had happened twelve years ago would serve only to exacerbate her condition. As soon as he thought she was healthy enough to handle it, they'd talk. This wasn't the kind of conversation he wanted to delay any longer than necessary.

She reached over and squeezed his upper

arm. "Hey, it's okay. These things happen when they're supposed to happen."

"Did I look sad?" Well, that was embarrassing.

"Kind of, yes. A muscle in your cheek has this tic..." Her voice trailed off as everything inside the car seemed to grow still. Even the radio had grown quiet, causing the silence to permeate every molecule of air between them.

All those years ago, she'd used to kiss that very spot on his cheek every time he'd retreated inside himself. He'd been the glue holding his family together—between his mom's ill health, his dad's gambling addiction and his younger brother's tendency to spend nights locked in a cell, someone had needed to keep a roof over their heads and food on the table. Natasha always knew when the weight of responsibility was beginning to crush him underfoot, and she used to tenderly place her lips against his cheek.

"Make a left turn in fifty feet," said the disembodied voice of the GPS. "Your destination will be on your right."

"Does any of this look familiar?" Jolted out of memory, he scanned the street as they turned onto it. She lived in a decent-looking neighborhood, a typical middle-class residential area. Inflatable Christmas decorations lay flat on a number of lawns, colorful fabric puddles waiting for nightfall so they could come to life. Other homes were decorated with strings of lights, plastic reindeer and garland streamers that rustled in the breeze. He'd grown up in Florida, but after a few years in the Midwest and farther north, in states that actually received snow in December, it was odd to reconcile inflatable snowman decor with green lawns and palm trees.

He noted the decreasing house numbers, then pulled the Suburban up alongside the curb in front of a row of attached condos. They were tall, boxy buildings, with beige siding and single-car garages. It looked like a few of the units were slightly wider than the others. A double staircase led from the ground level up to the main floor, and a set of sliding glass doors opened onto a small balcony on each top floor. The front yard of each wasn't much more than a bland, rectangular bit of grass with a young tree in the center.

"You're number thirty-seven, right? I think that's what I read on the paper." For some reason, he'd expected Natasha to live in a fancy Tuscan-style home, something with a three-car garage, a colonnaded porch, tall palm trees and a pool out back. Something more like the home she'd grown up in, a place that aligned more with her family's beliefs about wealth and social status.

"Thirty-nine, actually," she said, folding the papers back up. "I used to live in thirty-seven, but Hayley and I swapped units with our neighbors right before my launch, really lovely people. Thirty-seven is one of the slightly wider units with an extra bedroom, and since they had a baby on the way with two other children under three, we—" She froze midsentence. "How do I know that?"

"Dr. Olsen said your memory loss would be selective, remember? I'd say this is a good sign." He cut the engine and hopped out, then jogged around to the other side to open the door for her. "It's late afternoon, almost four o'clock. Will Hayley be home?"

Natasha squinted up at the condos, her gaze swinging between numbers thirty-seven and thirty-nine. "She…might be? If I've been missing, she's probably been staying with the neighbors. She stays there when I have overnight training or a conference to attend. In exchange, and for a bit of spending money, she babysits for Rania after school sometimes, so Rania can have a bit of personal time. With the baby, of course. Hayley got her babysitting certificate as soon as she turned twelve. The course fee was her birthday present." Her voice rose with excitement as she recalled details about her daughter.

Maybe yours, too, he told himself. "Your daughter sounds like quite the entrepreneur. Smart kid." He swallowed hard. That lump in his throat refused to go away. "Does she look after the kids in your current place or next door at the old place?"

Natasha didn't respond, but took the first flight of steps halfway up to unit thirty-nine before pausing. She remained still for a moment, then turned around and came back down. A small red mailbox was positioned on the outer wall next to the garage door, decorated with a gaudy gold-and-silver tinsel wreath that looked like it had come from a discount store. Natasha placed her hands on either side of the mailbox and lifted it off the wall. A strip of duct tape underneath held two house keys in place, which she removed before replacing the mailbox.

"Either place," she said. "And Hayley has her own set of keys to get inside, but… I remembered these were here."

"Another good sign." He rocked back and

forth on his heels as nervousness dug in further. As Natasha started to climb back up the steps, a large, silvery-gray mass of fur and muscle careened up the sidewalk, leaping toward her with massive front paws. "Look out!"

He lunged for the dog. Instead of shouting in alarm, Natasha laughed and leaned into the creature's awkward embrace. Its paws scrabbled against her legs and torso. As they greeted each other, the dog dropped back onto all fours and took small steps backward, punctuating its movements with short, terse barks.

"You know this dog?" Chris asked. "Something's clearly got him worked up."

"It's a she," Natasha said, ruffling her fingers along the fur at the dog's collar. She bent to read the tags. "Her name is Fin. Short for Infinity. She belongs to the neighbors."

"Infinity? Cute." Chris couldn't help but smile. "She has such an unusual coloring! I don't think I've seen it before."

"Silver Lab," Natasha said, trying to beckon the dog back to her waiting hands. "I love dogs, but I'm away too often to care for one myself. Maybe when Hayley's a little older."

"What's she doing on the loose?"

"She must have escaped from the backyard, or maybe Hayley let her out by accident. Not a problem. I'll let her back in the house so Rania doesn't come home and wonder where her dog has wandered off to." As Natasha crossed the driveway to her old condo, the dog followed after her, barking and whining. When she reached the steps, Infinity's whining grew stronger and her tail drooped. The dog placed her front paws on the bottom steps but refused to follow Natasha up.

Chris's heart squeezed at the sounds coming from the agitated canine. "Hey, something's not right here—don't you think? She seems worried."

Natasha reached the first landing and looked over the railing at him. Under different circumstances, he might have made a joke about the moment feeling like a scene out of *Romeo and Juliet*—after all, their families hadn't liked each other, just like that ill-fated couple's—but it would fall flat without Natasha's memories of the two of them. Based on the way her memories of Hayley and her home were pouring back into her brain, however, it wouldn't be long before she remembered him, too.

"She's probably just nervous about the kids," she said. "They can be loud, especially if Rania's youngest has a screaming tantrum. He's still learning not to pull on Fin's ears and tail—

oh, there I go again, remembering things. It's so strange—like one moment, there's nothing inside my head, and the next moment, there's too much and I have to let it out. Sorry. You probably don't care to know all these random facts I'm spilling. Long story short—the poor dog likely needs a quiet place to rest."

"If you say so." But the dog's whimpering increased to an all-out wail as Natasha climbed the remaining steps. The instant she inserted her key in the lock, Fin tore up the stairs, reaching Natasha just as she turned the key. Fin leaped up, grabbed Natasha's shirt in her teeth and yanked backward. Natasha stumbled back with a cry of surprise, her fingers brushing against the front door and sending it swinging inward just as a mighty pull from Fin dragged her down the first flight of stairs.

And then the front of the house exploded.

Natasha's breath came in ragged gasps as she clung to the dog's soft fur. Muffled sounds rang in her ears as she blinked away the dust and debris that obscured her vision.

"Tasha!" Chris barreled across the short space to reach her—how had she gotten on the ground?—and knelt by her side. "Are you all right? Does anything hurt?"

For a moment, she thought she felt the dog beneath her grow still, and her insides tightened. Then the large, furry body rolled underneath her and sneezed. *Thank You, Lord.* "I think Fin just saved my life," she said. Her words sounded strange, and her body felt worse than it had when she'd arrived at the hospital earlier, but that didn't matter. There was something very, very important she was forgetting. Something critical—

It returned to her in a flash.

"Hayley!" She pushed to her feet and stumbled toward the demolished staircase, not caring how much her body hurt. She'd climb the drainpipe or knock down the garage door to get inside if she had to, because if her daughter and those little ones had been inside the house during the explosion… "Hayley, can you hear me? I'm coming!"

Strong arms wrapped around her from behind and pulled her away from the smoking remains of the front entrance above them. Chunks of the door and the landing fell, but she didn't care. She'd find a way in. She'd break down the door at the back of the house, or—

"Tasha, no! It's not safe." Chris's breath across her neck made her pause. She stopped struggling against his grip. "Does Hayley have hair like yours? Curly? Reddish brown? A girl just came outside at your place."

Sure enough, the sound of feet pounding down the next-door steps was followed by her daughter's strained cries. "Mom? Mom! You're home!"

Natasha pulled free from Chris's grasp and opened her arms to embrace her daughter. She squeezed her tightly once, then held her out at arm's length. "You're all right? The others, too?"

Hayley nodded, her eyes wide and teary. "Yeah, we're fine. I just heard a boom and looked out the window and saw smoke. What happened? Where have you been?"

The reality of seeing her child alive and well sank in, and she clutched Hayley to her chest again.

"Mom, I can't breathe," Hayley said, her voice muffled. When she pulled away, the girl's eyes flicked to the side and back again. "Why didn't you tell me you'd be away overnight? It's not on our calendar. The Kaifs said you probably just forgot to write it down, but I know you don't forget that kind of thing and I was *freaking out*. Who's that?"

"Who?" Natasha followed her daughter's gaze to see Chris, standing back and staring at the two of them. He looked pale and shaken, but she suspected she looked even worse for wear. "Oh, that's Agent Barton from the FBI. He helped me when— You know what? It's a long story and I'll tell you after we get this all figured out." The poor Kaifs and their lovely home. A week from Christmas, no less! Could it have been a natural-gas leak? But she didn't smell mercaptan, the odorant that gas companies added to natural gas so that even the smallest leak could be immediately detected. Ruling that out, could it have been wiring gone wrong? She thanked God that the children hadn't been inside. She ushered Hayley, Chris and Fin into her own home, where they could keep an eye on Rania's children. The house felt strange and yet familiar at the same time. She needn't have worried about having a tree, because she'd clearly gone all out decorating for the holiday. A Christmas tree sat in the corner of the living room, tall enough to touch the ceiling, the branches so filled with lights and a random assortment of handmade ornaments that they bowed toward the floor. She didn't remember making them, but at the same time, they felt…right. As she took in the rest of the room, it was bizarre to see some things she recognized but others that looked out of place.

She was a stranger in her own skin, with nothing to grasp on to but thin, random memories like wispy strands of tinsel.

A bulletin board next to the refrigerator listed emergency contacts and neighbors' phone numbers—and a large calendar listed all of hers and Hayley's appointments in detail. She used her landline to call Rania while Chris made his own calls to the FBI and local police. With help on the way, Natasha sank into the living room's tan suede couch. Hayley returned to the floor to play with the children, who were oblivious to everything but the brightly colored plastic blocks and noise-making toys around them. Fin jumped up and placed her head and paws on Natasha's lap. She stroked the dog's shiny silver coat, grateful for her neighbors' intelligent pet.

"Fin must have known there was a problem," she murmured. "Dogs can sense danger that our limited human senses can't. Labradors are particularly intelligent."

Chris half stood and half sat against the arm of the couch, not fully committing one way or the other. It was similar to the pose he'd taken next to her hospital bed, as if he was preparing to bolt at any moment.

"I've heard that, as well. If she hadn't pulled

you away from the door… Well, as it was, the blast sent you both flying down the rest of the steps, but she took the hit for you. It's probably why you're not unconscious from another blow to your head. Fin deserves an entire bag of treats, if you ask me."

"Maybe two." She sighed, grateful indeed. "I just can't believe it. I've heard of natural-gas explosions happening without much warning, but the entire area would smell like rotten eggs from the mercaptan if that was the cause. Whatever it actually was, I thought newer homes like these would be more secure, less prone to issues."

"When did you say you switched apartments?" Chris's voice was soft but carried an undercurrent of tension. "Recently?"

She nodded. "Right before I left on the Orion mission."

"And the move is on record?"

"No, not yet. It was a bit of a last-minute decision since the Kaifs had only just started telling people about their pregnancy and I was leaving the following week. We figured we'd fill out the official paperwork when I got back, and got approval from the homeowner's association for the whole thing. It's been easy enough to simply hand off mail to each other, but I don't see why that's important right now."

"Don't you?"

She shook her head, then winced. It still hurt. She might be running high on adrenaline from what had happened, but both her mind and body had taken a massive beating today. She needed to take it easy.

"Natasha," Chris said impatiently. "Think about it. How many attempts on your life have there been today? You're on record as living next door. Someone thinks that's your home. That was no natural-gas explosion. That was a bomb, and it was intended to kill you."

FOUR

"Natasha? Hold on." An hour later, Chris jogged across the driveway to where Natasha stood with her daughter, each of them holding large tote bags. Hayley's looked ready to overflow, while Natasha's looked nearly empty. Natasha also held a cell phone to her ear. Where had she gotten a cell phone? "What are you doing over here? You planning on going somewhere? And whose phone is that?"

Natasha pulled the phone an inch away from her head. "I borrowed it from Officer Lee. I'm calling a cab. We can't stay here tonight—they already told me that after taking our statements—so I'm going to get us a room in town."

"And how do you propose to do that? You don't have an ID or credit cards or any bank information to withdraw cash."

For a moment, she looked stricken—but she recovered quickly, setting her lips in a firm line. "I'm sure NASA will take care of it for me. I'll ask them for help. It's not like they can't get a night's room rate back out of my paycheck."

Chris resisted the urge to roll his eyes. Yes, she could certainly do that, but it didn't make sense to let her fend for herself when he and the FBI could help. In fact, he didn't think it wise to leave her alone overnight—that would be irresponsible of him, considering the repeated attempts on her life. Whether the explosion in the condo was the result of an incompetent contractor or a bomb would be determined shortly, but he didn't want to take any chances. *I mean*, he corrected himself, *the FBI doesn't want to take any chances.* He didn't know much about her work beyond that the government considered her and her fellow crew members national assets, and that they'd been testing new technology that could result in a massive breakthrough for the United States space program. He didn't know much about space and scientific research, either, but no FBI agent could afford to be ignorant of the "Space Race" between the United States and the former Soviet Union during the mid to late twentieth century. And really, no one had truly won that race. To get anyone up to the International Space Station these days, Soyuz spacecraft were launched out of Kazakhstan, a country located on Russia's southern border. Chris could certainly see how new technology that allowed American spacecraft to launch regularly again from within US borders would be highly coveted and critically important to the country's future.

"I'll take you into town and get you set up," he offered. He held his hand out for the phone, which she dropped into his palm with a little more aggression than necessary. He didn't blame her. With so many missing pieces of memory, losing what should have been a safe place to rest and recover had to be frustrating. "And I know you probably don't want to hear this right now, but you'll have to get used to having a tail for a while."

"A tail?" She blinked at him in confusion, then glanced over to where her neighbor was gathering her children and Fin into her car. The Kaifs hadn't even been allowed to pack a bag, what with forensic teams crawling through their home to search for the source of the explosion. Chris felt bad for the family—as if having their home destroyed wasn't bad enough; it was even worse to have it happen only one week before Christmas, and with such young children.

"Someone following you around, a detail watching outside your hotel room, that kind of thing."

"Of course." She groaned and ran her hand down the side of her face. "I knew that. Sorry—I'm still feeling jumbled. It's as if someone put a whisk into my brain and scrambled everything around."

He reached across and took both her tote bag and Hayley's. "I'm not surprised. Let's get you settled for the evening so you can rest."

"Hayley has homework to do, too—don't you, sweetheart?" Natasha stroked her daughter's hair. The girl cringed and her cheeks turned a light shade of pink, appropriately embarrassed by her mother's show of affection in public.

Typical twelve-year-old, Chris thought. His stomach twisted as he watched the mother-daughter interaction. Hayley certainly had her mother's bright blue eyes, and deep auburn hair, but her nose and ears… Chris touched his own nose before realizing what he was doing. Part of him hoped his suspicions were incorrect, because how could Natasha have kept something like this from him all these years? *You deleted all her emails and refused all forms of communication*, he reminded himself. But that didn't excuse her from telling him before they'd broken the engagement, if she'd been pregnant with his child. And if this girl was his daughter, he didn't want to miss another moment with her. He'd find a way to make up lost years, one way or the other.

But learning the truth was impossible until Natasha's memories returned, no matter how desperately he wanted to know it now.

"I'll double-check with the teams and make sure they don't need anything else from either one of us. Hang on." He jogged back inside and returned Officer Lee's phone, then checked with the local police and the FBI's Evidence Response team to ensure that they'd received what they needed from Natasha and Hayley. Back outside, he directed mother and daughter to his vehicle. They drove in relative silence into town, the tension occasionally punctuated by an emphatic preteen sigh from the back seat.

By the time he'd set up Natasha and Hayley in a hotel, the tension between mother and daughter seemed to have grown to an all-out cold war. He suspected Hayley resented being forced to leave home when it wasn't even her house that had exploded, especially after having her world in upheaval for the past twenty-four hours while her mom was missing.

As soon as Natasha used the hotel key card to unlock the room, Hayley stormed inside and flopped into an armchair in the corner, arms crossed. Natasha nodded her thanks to Chris and looked ready to follow, but he couldn't let her go just yet—not when there was so much still left unsaid after the events of the day.

"Can I talk to you for a moment?" He looked past her into the room. She followed his gaze, then pulled the door shut behind her, leaving the two of them to talk in the hallway. "We didn't finish our conversation earlier."

Natasha pressed her lips together and shook her head. "About what? You know, before today I could count on one hand the number of times I'd talked to police officers. Now I think I need three hands just to count them all, and that's not including FBI. I'm tired, and I'm trying really hard not to think about the fact that there's at least twelve hours in my history that's unaccounted for, on top of my missing memories. So if you want to rehash everything I told the other officers—"

"No! Of course not." He hooked his thumbs

in his waistband and stepped back. Maybe he'd chosen the wrong time for this. She really did need to rest, but it felt dishonest to continue interacting with her on this case without answering the question she'd asked him back in the hospital. She had a right to know, and hopefully when her memories returned, she'd appreciate that he'd been up front with her. "It's about me. Well, you and me. Remember when you asked if we knew each other apart from what's happened today?"

Her eyes widened, and she ran her fingers through the ends of her hair. "There's something familiar about you, but I can't put my finger on it. Are you saying that we do know each other?"

"Yes, but—" His next words stalled on his tongue. How did you tell someone that they'd broken your heart over a decade ago when they didn't even remember your name? He tried again. No-nonsense honesty seemed like the best approach. "Natasha, the thing is—"

"It's bad, isn't it." It wasn't a question. "We know each other, but it's not a good situation."

Perceptive, this woman. Probably why she makes such a good astronaut. "Something like that."

She nodded, lowered her eyes for a moment

and then looked up at him sharply. "I don't want to know."

"Excuse me?"

"Don't tell me. Not yet, anyway. When this all blows over and my head feels less scrambled, then we can talk about it. I've had enough of bad news and jumbled truths today. Maybe I'll even be able to handle it tomorrow, but I'm so tired. Every new question sends a fresh wave of panic through my system. And let's face it—the doctor told me to take it easy. Thanks to the explosion back at the condo, I think I've done the exact opposite."

She made a very good point, but it still ate at his conscience. "Only if you're certain. I think you're going to want to know, but I also don't want to tax your mental faculties further, and you're right—the doctor did tell you to rest. You're not supposed to be falling down stairs or doing mentally challenging activities like giving witness statements. I can only imagine the extra strain."

"Thank you for understanding. We'll talk tomorrow, okay? And thanks for everything today, Agent Barton." He almost corrected her, but she smiled and winked as she opened the door to her hotel room. "I mean, Chris."

"No need to thank me, Ms. Stark. Just doing

my job. I'll be right next door, so please don't hesitate if you need anything or have any kind of concern."

"You're staying?" She raised both eyebrows. "That seems a little over the top—don't you think?"

"Not at all. Your safety is my primary concern." He swallowed hard as a warm smile lit up her features. "Hope you're able to get some solid rest, both of you."

She closed the door, and he ran his hand down his face, then slumped against the wall. They'd avoided a painful conversation for one night, but tomorrow wasn't far off. He only hoped that she felt better by then and had regained some additional memories. Having bits and pieces come back to her today was a good sign, but his insides still roiled at the thought of her looking at him with that same dismissive, disgusted expression as she had twelve years ago. He'd hoped to never endure heartbreak and embarrassment like that again, and had made his way across the country to avoid ever seeing her and returning to that moment. But now here he was on the other side of a door from her, experiencing a strange and unwelcome surge of emotion that made him feel like a teenager again. And in a cruel twist of irony, she didn't remember him at all.

Should he even confront her about Hayley? If Natasha did feel better in the morning, whether she remembered him or not, that would be quite the bombshell to drop during an already difficult time.

No, he'd wait for her to bring it up again. The moment she did, he'd speak the truth and ask her outright if Hayley was his daughter. But if she didn't say anything, he'd let it be until her memories fully returned.

Either way, he knew one thing for certain: he couldn't afford to fall for Natasha Stark again…despite what his heart seemed to want.

Inside the NASA physician's office the next morning, Natasha looked at the clock on the wall and groaned. Eight thirty in the morning. She'd slept nearly eight hours last night, and she still felt like she needed at least eight more.

"Everything looks up to snuff," Dr. Jarvis said, typing her notes into the exam room computer. "You're doing well on the physical end of things. I agree with the assessment Dr. Olsen gave you at the hospital in terms of your memory loss. I don't think it's exacerbated by your recovery statistics from returning to Earth, but

I advise that you try not to tax your memory too much on purpose. Allow thoughts to come back naturally as opposed to straining for them."

Natasha rubbed her arms, which were covered in goose bumps from the chilly air in the exam room. "Certain words or images seem to bring bits and pieces back. Like when Dr. Olsen mentioned Hayley or when I saw my condo. Would that be considered taxing it on purpose, or is that a more passive method of recovery?"

Dr. Jarvis leaned back in her chair and swiveled to face Natasha. "Actually, if that's working for you and not causing headaches or any of the fogginess you described, then I think it's a great way to work on your recovery. I'd be careful and take it easy, of course—and I'd like to see you back here tomorrow just for a quick update. In fact...have you talked to any of the other crew members since this happened?"

Natasha shook her head. "I can't remember their names, so how would I have spoken to them?"

Dr. Jarvis smiled. "I have a suggestion. You and the crew were aboard the Orion together for six months. Why not visit them and see if speaking with them jogs any memories?

Ask a few questions about yourself and listen to their responses. Don't think too hard about their answers. Just absorb what they tell you and allow it to strengthen those synaptic connections naturally, or not. Based on what you've told me, this is my best suggestion to try regaining some sense of self. I'll call down to HR and have one of the staff print off some files for you with crew photos, addresses, that kind of thing."

Natasha thanked Dr. Jarvis and exited the exam room after the doctor. Chris sat in the waiting room, his leg bouncing anxiously on the edge of a chair. He sat hunched over, hands clasped, but his head swiveled in casual observation. If she didn't know he was an FBI agent, she'd assume he was a nervous patient. An attractive, too-eye-catching-for-his-own-good patient. She hoped he didn't catch her staring, but at the same time, she couldn't look away.

"Ready to go?" He stood as soon as he noticed her, which didn't take long. Her heart skipped a beat as they locked eyes. He looked at her with such concern, such sincerity, that she knew without a shadow of a doubt that they had some kind of personal history. She couldn't remember the last time another person had looked at her that way—not that she remembered much of anything right now. Under different circumstances, she might have welcomed his attention. But he'd made it perfectly clear last night that whatever history they had wasn't positive, and that meant despite the brightness and warmth she felt when she looked at him, she'd feel differently as soon as her memories returned. Why hadn't her memories of him been jogged when she looked at him the way they had with Hayley or her neighbor? *Selective memory, indeed.*

"Dr. Jarvis is grabbing some personnel files for me," she said as he walked over. "She suggested that I visit my Orion mission crew members and see if that jogs any memories."

He ran his hand along his jaw, rough with day-old stubble. "That sounds like a good idea."

They waited in awkward silence until one of Dr. Jarvis's receptionists brought over a file folder. Natasha took it and flipped through the papers inside. Photos of two women and two men stared back at her, but none of their images triggered any specific memories. *Maybe not being able to remember Chris isn't so strange after all*, she thought. Especially considering what Dr. Jarvis had pointed out—she and these four crew members had lived in extremely close quarters for six months, as recently as three weeks ago. If she knew any other person as well as she knew herself, it would be them. She read through all the notes as bits and pieces of her life were unlocked in flashes. It seemed that experiences were coming back easily—images of where she'd been, things she'd seen—but *people* were her brain's sticking point. She'd spent six months in space with these people, testing the spacecraft and a new life-support module in hopes that it could soon be used to carry a crew all the way to Mars and back. On the International Space Station, an astronaut could go an entire day without seeing another person—but on the much smaller Orion, the crew inevitably would end up knowing more personal details about one another than they could possibly want.

"Who would you like to visit first?" Chris pulled one of the papers out, but Natasha snatched it back and replaced it in the folder. "What?"

"I realize these are just general info sheets, but it's still classified information. Do you have clearance to view NASA personnel files?"

"I'm FBI."

"That's not the same thing, and you know it."

Chris sighed. He gestured for her to follow

him and they exited the building to head to his vehicle. "This place has high security," he commented as they passed through the gates to leave Kennedy Space Center. "I don't recall reading about all this security when we reviewed government facilities back in Quantico."

"It's new," she said, realizing with delight that she had the answer. "It was all installed once the Orion project received the go-ahead. Just in case, you know? It's not like NASA has been a popular site for infiltration or terrorism, but when you're working on new technology that could literally change the world, you don't take any chances."

Chris grunted in agreement as they pulled onto the highway. "Guess if I need to hide you away someplace, we can send you here. But hopefully there'll be no more reason for that."

Natasha swiveled to check the road behind them. The tension in her shoulders dropped at seeing no one there but a little gray Toyota with an elderly woman at the wheel. "Have you heard anything about what happened at the condo?" She noticed his jaw grow tense. "Or should I not have asked?"

"No, it's fine." He checked his blind spot. "I know you wanted it to be faulty wiring, Tasha, or some other innocuous cause, but it wasn't. I got a call while you were getting checked up. Someone deliberately set a bomb in the condo, probably assuming that unit was yours. The FBI considers that attempted murder."

Natasha's throat grew tight. "It doesn't make sense. I don't have anything that anyone would want."

"That's what the FBI is going to try to figure out, but for now you need to focus on talking to your crew members and not dwelling on the negative. It'll only exhaust you and damage your recovery, correct?"

She nodded. "It's one thing to tell me you're going to handle it, but it's quite another to tell me that someone obviously wants me dead and nobody knows why."

"Not for long—I promise. I'm going to figure it out. Hopefully as you get your memories back, you'll have a few ideas of your own."

She opened the folder on her lap and studied the profile of the crew member they were headed to visit first: Dr. Jeremy Evans, specialist in biochemistry and bioagriculture. He was in his late forties and had a long list of achievements to his name, including three previous space flights. He'd been in charge of agricultural experiments on the Orion, particularly as a part of testing the new Deep Space Habitat system. Figuring out the most effective way to grow plants without Earth's gravity and natural systems was critical for determining methods to keep astronauts fed while out in space for long durations. Fresh food was rare and highly coveted on missions.

Chris and Natasha pulled up in front of a quaint bungalow with white siding and an impressive lawn. Neatly trimmed hedges and elaborate flower beds rivaled any Flower & Garden Festival display that Epcot in Orlando offered. A delicate Christmas display of white wooden reindeer, posed as if grazing in the garden, created a sense of joyous wonder.

"It's beautiful," she murmured as Chris parked the Suburban. She inhaled deeply to enjoy the blend of floral scents and fresh grass as she walked up the driveway. "I wonder if he maintains this himself. I'd love to have a flower garden, but the condo doesn't have much in the way of green space."

Chris turned to her with a clear question on his lips—they parted as his eyebrows rose—but he seemed to think better of it and turned away. "I've never been much of a green thumb myself," he said, then rapped on the front door.

After no response, Chris knocked again. “Dr. Evans?”

Still no response. Natasha walked back down the path to the driveway and peered around the edge of the house. “The garage door is open, and there’s a car inside. He must be home.”

“Resting? Taking a dog for a walk?” Chris leaned over the porch railing to look in the front window. “I don’t see him. Would he even be home? Not at NASA or elsewhere?”

“We’re supposed to take it easy for the first few weeks after coming home. I guess it’s possible that he’s out, but I don’t think Dr. Jarvis would send me out to visit my crew if she didn’t know they’d be home. Our time is quite rigidly scheduled, especially in the months before and after a mission. I have Evans’s phone number on the personnel sheet. I can leave a message and come back later.”

Before Natasha could stop him, Chris placed his hand on the door handle and pressed the lever down. The door swung open, unlocked. “Dr. Evans?” he called.

Natasha stuck her head through the doorway. A chill ran down the back of her spine as a sense of wrongness washed over her.

“Chris, something’s not right.” The pleasant floral scent from outdoors gave way to a sharp, coppery smell that made her cringe. She exhaled through her nose several times, trying to escape the conflux of smells as she stepped farther into the house. The smell grew even stronger as she moved through the living room and toward the kitchen, and in an instant it was as though she'd been kicked in the stomach. She knew that smell, all too familiar from the events of the day before. *Blood.*

"Dr. Evans?" Chris called behind her. Natasha heard the sound of his weapon sliding out of its holster, and he placed his hand in front of her to stop her from moving. He met her eyes and silently communicated that she stay positioned behind him. They moved past the kitchen and into the main hallway, Chris poking his head around each corner to check for threats.

Finally, they reached the last room at the end of the hall. The door stood slightly ajar, and Natasha recognized the hum of electronics coming from inside. It had to be Dr. Evans's office. With his free hand, Chris pushed the door open. From where Natasha stood behind Chris, it looked as though they'd found Dr. Evans. She could see the back of his head, tilted to the side as he sat in his desk chair.

"Dr. Evans?" In front of her, Chris shook his head. "What?"

And then she could see more, and it struck her. The smell, the awkward angle of his head. The arm dangling from the other side of the chair, fingers extended and gently curled, with a gun beneath his fingertips. As though it had dropped from his hand…

Chris entered the room and walked around the front of the chair, his expression calm. A muscle moved in his jaw as he holstered his weapon. He flicked his eyes up to meet hers, then shook his head.

Bile rose up the back of Natasha's throat, and for the first time since she'd learned she had amnesia, she felt grateful that she didn't have a stronger memory of Dr. Evans. Would she be crippled by grief for her fellow crew member? They were probably friends, and the loss would hit her later. Right now she needed to stay calm. Remain logical. Think it through like an astronaut would when confronted with a problem.

"What happened?" she whispered, though she wasn't sure she even wanted to know.

Chris pointed to the gun on the floor, the side of Dr. Evans's head and then the far side of the room. Natasha gasped and slammed her back against the wall in the hallway, taking deep breaths to ease her racing pulse. She closed her eyes, trying to erase the image of blood spatter on the lilac wallpaper.

"I'm sorry," Chris said, his voice soft as he made his way back to her. "But it looks like Dr. Evans took his own life."

FIVE

Chris watched Natasha closely as the information sank in. It certainly looked like the astronaut had taken his own life—and there was nothing about the scene that appeared out of place or unusual. No signs of forced entry at the front door, no indication of struggle. He had a strong hunch that the forensic team would come to the same conclusion, but something about it didn't sit right.

"Do you remember Dr. Evans?" he asked after ending his call to the FBI to report what they'd found. "What he was like, his temperament?"

Natasha remained still. To anyone else, it might look like she was cold and dispassionate—but Chris perceived otherwise. She certainly was having difficulty processing the scene, but her astronaut training had kicked in to keep her outwardly calm even while she might be screaming inside. This wasn't good for her mental health, but only she could make the call on whether she needed to back off and rest.

"I can take you back to the hotel," he said. "If you need to take a break, say the word. I can communicate the details of the case via phone rather than standing here."

"I'm fine" came her terse reply. "I'll *be* fine. I just… You don't expect to see something like that. I've learned and participated in simulations and studied diagrams of a thousand and one ways to die in outer space, but I guess I never considered the possibility of dying here on Earth instead. Six months in space and then…suicide? After all that, after the marvels we saw…"

"You remember your time on the Orion?"

"Not really." She rubbed the heels of her hands into her eyes. "Not the details, anyway. But cognitively I know that being out there changes a person. Seeing the entire world like that, as one cohesive whole rather than the small slices of humanity and nature we interact with day to day. It reminds you that there's a bigger picture. That those everyday troubles we have are nothing compared to the vastness of the universe. God's creation is so spectacular."

God? She stood only a few feet away from where a fellow astronaut had ended his own life and she still said God's creation was spectacular? "So, that's still a thing for you, then? The God stuff?"

She looked at him quizzically, and he could have smacked himself. They weren't supposed to be talking about the past.

"Yes, it is. And I don't appreciate your tone of voice."

"I'm sorry—you're right. Not my place." Her eyes narrowed at him, and he sighed. "I'm not trying to sound patronizing—I promise. Did you want to go wait in the vehicle for the forensic team to get here? You don't need to be near this scene any longer than necessary. I'm concerned for your mental health, to be quite honest."

"I'll be all right. I just can't believe that he would have done something like this. It doesn't make sense." She looked over her shoulder into the office before Chris could stop her. He watched the way she swallowed nervously, and he felt a strange urge to fold her into his arms. He gripped his wrists behind his back to try to eliminate the impulse. "Someone is going to have to tell his family…" Her voice trailed off as her eyes fixated on something inside the room.

Chris immediately followed her gaze. "What is it?"

"That photo." She pointed. "On his desk."

"To the left or the right?"

"The right. The one with him and the woman."

"We can take a closer look." He started toward it, but she didn't follow. "You okay?"

She shook her head and stared at the floor. "I can't come in there. I just can't. I'm sorry."

He understood completely. "You're not a robot, Natasha. It's okay to be upset. Hang on—let me grab some tools from the truck." Chris took off down the hall and returned moments later with a plastic bag and a pair of disposable gloves. "Anything in that room could be considered evidence, so I'll bring it out for you to have a look at, but you can't touch it." He used the gloves to remove the photo from the desk and held it up for Natasha to examine. "Do you recognize the woman?"

"Yes, I know her. From the personnel sheets of the crew members. That's Cobie May. She was an air-force pilot and tactical aviation specialist before being selected as an astronaut candidate."

Chris flipped the photo around to see for himself. It wasn't a great shot, but it was full of life and motion. He figured the woman for midthirties, and her arm was flung over Dr. Evans's shoulders as the photographer caught them both midlaugh. Cobie May leaned forward in the photo as if unable to control the force of her laughter, and Dr. Evans had eyes only for the woman beside him. It was the kind of candid shot a friend might take at an informal social gathering, a shot typical of social-media posts—but who these days printed off a candid, slightly blurry photo and framed it?

"They look cozy," he said. "Any particular reason he'd have this photo of the two of them on his desk, front and center? And no photos of the rest of you?"

Natasha examined it again. Finally, her lips parted and she nodded as though in disbelief. "Yes, there is. He and May are an item! That explains the HR notation in Evans's file. They fell in love on the Orion and started seeing each other seriously after we returned home. Chris, why would a man in love who's happy with his job and has a beautiful home like this just...kill himself? It makes even less sense."

She was right—there was no logical reason for a stable individual with strong social support and new love to have taken his own life, which left two other plausible reasons for the man's death. Either the woman he thought was the love of his life had turned out not to be the kind of person he thought she was—a situation Chris was very well acquainted with—or the man hadn't taken his own life at all.

"Natasha, in the past forty-eight hours, there have been repeated attempts on your life. And now we're standing in a house with a fellow astronaut who appears to have taken his own. Even if the forensics prove otherwise, and I'm not saying they will, this doesn't sit right."

"What *are* you saying?" She paled.

"I'm saying that this might have been set up. I know it doesn't look like it at first glance, but I don't think we can rule out murder. Whoever came after you didn't succeed. So what if they went after Dr. Evans instead?"

At Chris's words, Natasha swayed on her feet, then stumbled down the hallway. She had to get away from the smell of blood, from the mental picture of Dr. Evans, from seeing another gun inexplicably close to someone's hand. Yesterday she'd come out of unconsciousness to find a gun by her own hand. Could what happened to Dr. Evans have been what happened to her if Chris hadn't come along? Was she intended to be the first victim?

"Did I do this?" The words scraped the back of her throat as she burst out the front door and dropped to her knees on the grass, hands braced on her thighs and head bowed. "Did I cause this to happen?"

And then Chris was beside her, his strong hands gripping her shoulders. He squeezed gently to bring her back to reality, grounding her from the overwhelming grief and guilt that threatened to consume her.

"Did *you* order a hit on Dr. Evans?"

She grimaced. "What? Of course not."

"Exactly. Whatever happened to him in there, it's not your fault. There's no scenario here where blame falls on your shoulders."

"That could have been me. Or…or what if I tried to kill myself, too? Maybe I failed and ended up on the side of the road. Maybe we caught a rare virus, or got space sickness like the crew of Apollo 8, or are all having psychotic breakdowns—"

"Is that likely?"

"No, but—"

He gripped her face between his palms,

forcing eye contact. "You know very well that neither of those things is true. What is true, however, is that your life was in danger yesterday, and when we place that factual information next to the scene here, it's troubling. I'd rather we not spend more time out in the open like this than necessary. We're going to get into the Suburban now and leave the scene for the forensic teams to deal with. Do you understand?"

She nodded. Warmth spread from the tips of his fingers across her cheeks, soothing the flood of nerves and adrenaline that coursed through her body. Of all the people in the FBI who could have ended up on her case, she was immensely grateful that Chris had been the one to find her. His presence calmed her in a way she was sure she'd never felt before.

"Thank you," she said as he helped her to her feet. Once she'd situated herself in the vehicle, Chris dropped the folder of personnel sheets on her lap. "What's this for?"

"I'm going to take you back to NASA. The security there is extremely high, so you'll be safe. But I need an address from you first."

"What address?"

He adjusted his rearview mirror and began backing out of the driveway. "Cobie May's address. I want to get to her place so I can talk to her before the local police make the connection and head out there. She's as much a national asset as you are, and I don't want them scaring her and risk shutting down open dialogue. Honestly, I have no idea if they'd even try talking to her, but I still want to get to her first."

"Then I'm coming with you."

"No, you're not."

"Yes, I am. Are you going to tell her that her boyfriend is dead? Do you want to handle that conversation?"

He pressed the brake, stopping the vehicle while it hung halfway out of the driveway. "This is a federal investigation, and I can choose to withhold or provide the information as I deem it necessary."

"Doesn't matter." She opened the file, found Cobie May's address and punched it into the GPS. "She'll be devastated, and it'll be easier on her if there's a familiar face around."

"You remember her?"

"She knows me. I can offer the kind of comfort that a complete stranger simply can't."

Chris ran his hand through his hair, then gripped the steering wheel tight enough to cause his knuckles to pale. He exhaled through his nose, slow and deliberate, like he was trying to make up his mind about how to respond. Tension crept into Natasha's shoulders, but she wasn't backing down on this. It would be incredibly insensitive to not be there for a close coworker, regardless of the state of her own memories about the woman.

"All right," he finally said. "I see your point, and technically speaking, you're still my responsibility. Cobie May might also be more willing to answer my questions with a familiar face around. The more comfortable someone is, the more likely they are to cooperate."

She'd won, but the victory rang a little hollow. Was that all he saw her as? A responsibility? *And why should I expect him to see me any other way?* She was being foolish to think that they had some kind of connection, no matter how attractive she found him on the outside, and no matter how appealing his nature so far. He'd made it perfectly clear that whatever had happened between them in the past hadn't ended well, and inevitably she'd remember what that was, and then what? At that point, she might find herself heading for the hills, so to speak, and demanding a new FBI handler. For now, though, he seemed like the most stable thing in her life—aside from Hayley.

She thanked God that Hayley hadn't been

harmed yesterday and that the FBI had deemed it safe for her to attend school today. Schools in Titusville had decent security, and all the teachers were well trained regarding what to do in case of an emergency. Natasha had every confidence in the school's ability to keep her daughter safe in the classroom.

As Chris pulled the rest of the way out of the driveway, Natasha gazed out her passenger window—and did a double take as they passed a parked navy blue Range Rover.

"Chris!" she hissed as she twisted in her seat, wincing at the sudden movement. "The Range Rover!"

Chris checked his rearview again. "I don't see it. Your side or mine?"

"It was parked. We just passed it on my side."

"Could you tell if anyone was inside?"

"No." Her heart began to pound again. "But are all Range Rover windows tinted that dark? Maybe it's a coincidence. Or a different vehicle."

"Do you really believe that?" His tone had grown flat and serious. "I'll call it in. The forensic team should be almost to Dr. Evans's house. I don't want to double back with you in the vehicle. I won't intentionally put you in danger."

"It's a little late for that, don't you think?"

He bristled at her tone, obviously agitated. "What makes you say that? I'd never put you in danger on purpose, and I don't appreciate what you're implying."

"No, that's not what I meant. Look behind us." A rush of fear shot through her as the front bumper of the Range Rover stuck out from behind a parked car a block back and pulled onto the road. "Maybe it's not the same—"

The words stalled on her tongue as the vehicle revved its engine and sped toward them.

SIX

"The forensic team should be seconds away," Chris growled, feeling a surge of anger at seeing the Range Rover in his mirror again. Seriously, did this individual never give up? As the vehicle approached at an unsafe speed, he noted the large dent in the front passenger side. That had to be where it had clipped them yesterday.

"I thought you said the police were coming!" Natasha groaned.

"They are. They should be here any second."

"But we're in a residential area and it's gaining on us." Natasha punched numbers on the Bluetooth system. "What if a child or animal walks into the road? They could kill someone at that speed. I'm calling the police again to update them on what's going on."

As the call connected, the Range Rover

pulled up close enough to tap their bumper. The SUV lurched forward, and Chris had to make a split-second decision. Instead of staying on the residential straightaway, he took the next side street to go west, heading toward I-95, the nearest major highway. He needed to draw their pursuer out of the suburbs. Natasha was right. Driving at high speeds near homes and schools was a recipe for disaster.

Finally, the female dispatcher's voice came through the Suburban's speakers. Chris didn't wait for her to finish before relaying their plight.

"This is Special Agent Barton. I need backup on Palm Avenue heading toward I-95 via South Street. That same Range Rover that ran me off the road yesterday is going for a repeat in the middle of a school zone. There should be forensic and police teams already en route to the residence of NASA specialist Dr. Evans—redirect some of those officers to come toward me. I want this guy caught."

"Yes, sir." Dispatch disconnected, and Chris focused on the road ahead. He took another left turn as the Range Rover drew close to attempt another slam on their bumper, but Chris yanked the wheel and pulled them out of the way at the moment of impact. The Range Rover swerved, the driver having pulled too sharply to make the hit. The Range Rover swung from side to side as the driver tried to regain control, but on a narrow suburban street there was little room to maneuver. It clipped the edge of a parked sedan, swerved right and fishtailed into the edge of another car. The car's bumper crumpled, and the Range Rover's rear wheels lifted off the pavement at the force of the hit. Chris slowed the Suburban, waiting to see what the driver would do next. Seconds ticked by, and the vehicle remained motionless.

"That looked painful," Natasha said. "Do you think that hit was enough to convince them to back off?"

If the driver had been injured or incapacitated, Chris could pull over, make the arrest and stabilize the driver until help arrived—but the moment he jammed the Suburban's shifter into Park and unbuckled his seat belt, the Range Rover fired up again, backed away from the crumpled car and began to attempt a three-point turn in the narrow street.

As Chris opened his door, he heard the approach of police sirens. Backup had arrived, but they might not make it before the driver escaped. Chris wasn't about to waste this opportunity.

"Stay here," he shouted at Natasha as he jumped out of the Suburban, weapon drawn.

"Chris, no!" Natasha called. He hoped she'd listen to him and stay inside.

"FBI!" he shouted at the Range Rover, which had begun to reverse down the road. "Stop and exit the vehicle!"

The driver didn't stop—instead he sped up in his turn and swerved the vehicle backward, slamming into a stop sign and pushing the metal pole over. Then the driver revved the engine and took off in the opposite direction.

"Too late," Chris groaned. He jogged back to the Suburban and updated dispatch with the direction the suspect had fled. Moments later police cars with flashing lights and sirens turned the corner and headed away from their vehicle, in pursuit of the Range Rover.

"They'll catch him this time for sure," Natasha said. "He can't be far."

"Let's hope so." Chris drummed his fingers on the steering wheel. Impatience ate at his insides, compelling him to turn the Suburban around and join in the pursuit—but a high-speed chase was not the place to bring

Natasha. Let the local police handle it; they had multiple vehicles, could coordinate their approach and stood a much better chance of catching the suspect without him bringing a protected individual directly into the fray.

He felt Natasha's gaze on him. He didn't want to look at her. Adrenaline coursed too hot through his veins, and he didn't trust himself not to blurt out his question about Hayley. He was hungry for a small victory, for at least one sensible answer about everything going on, but now was not the time.

"Do you want to join the chase?" She leaned back in her seat and rested her elbow on the window ledge. "Don't let me stop you. I'll stay in the car."

How did she know what he was thinking? "The police will handle it."

"What are we going to do, then?"

This time he heard the anxiety that *she* had to be feeling. Managing the stress on her was of more importance than soothing his ego, which meant he needed to calm down and stop thinking about himself and how he wanted to react. This woman had been through enough, and forgetting that could compromise the investigation into why she'd disappeared in the first place. The sooner her memories returned, the sooner she'd have information on those missing hours.

"I'm going to keep doing my job," he said. He pulled them back onto the road. "We have another astronaut to visit. Forensics will deal with Dr. Evans, the local police will catch our pursuer, and I still need to figure out who could have potentially kidnapped a NASA mission specialist and dumped her on the side of the road twenty-four hours later with enough mental and physical trauma to cause severe, selective amnesia—not to mention that gun in your hand. Evans's death puts this in a whole different light, regardless of whether forensics thinks it looks like suicide or not. You and I both know that something isn't right here, and we're going to figure out the truth."

"You'll still let me come with you?"

"If the scene looks sketchy when we get there or if there are any warning signs, you're back in the vehicle and I'm taking you to NASA for lockdown. Understand?"

He met her eyes and waited for her to nod in agreement. "Thank you."

Chris exhaled slowly, regretting that he'd looked at her at all. Her eyes were so beautifully blue, like a Florida sky on a day without a single cloud in sight, and he knew that if he wasn't careful, he'd lose himself in their endless clarity.

She broke the moment first, then clasped her hands in her lap and fell silent as they drove. It was just as well—it meant Chris could focus on tuning into the police frequency to receive the updates on the pursuit of the Range Rover.

Minutes later, the final verdict came in. *Suspect lost.*

A BOLO remained out for the vehicle in question, but the pursuit had been a failure. The Range Rover had gained a head start on them and vanished. The police would continue to search the city for it, but until more eyewitness reports came in, they'd have a hard time tracking it down.

"Cobie May definitely doesn't have a green thumb," Natasha remarked as they pulled into a short driveway in front of a two-story home with a shabby-looking yard and a few yellowed shrubs—a sure sign of neglect that contrasted strongly with the lush gardens and holiday display at their previous stop. Only one area on the property stood out from the dry lawn, and there was no mistaking whose hand had been at work. "Looks like Dr. Evans was starting to take care of it for her, though."

Chris marked the direction of Natasha's

gaze. A small flower bed next to the front door was filled with a beautiful arrangement of planted flowers and neatly trimmed shrubs. A half-hearted attempt at Christmas decor came in the form of a large pine wreath covered in gaudy, red-and-gold ribbons that hung on the front door.

"Now it makes even less sense," Chris remarked. "I'd been turning over a theory about a bad breakup as we drove here, but if they'd had a nasty end to their relationship, surely May would have removed the plants that reminded her of him."

He headed up the driveway but paused when he realized that Natasha hadn't followed him. Turning around, he saw her standing next to the Suburban, staring without seeing.

"Tasha? You all right?"

It took a moment for her to respond, but when she did, she shook her head slowly. "I'm not sure. It feels like… I think I can remember Cobie. We're good friends. I remember her telling me about the first time she realized that she and Dr. Evans could be more than friends—she said it wasn't like falling in love the way you'd think, with butterflies and blushes and such, so much as she just woke up one morning and knew that life without him by her side would be incomplete."

Chris swallowed hard at the sudden lump in his throat. He understood that sentiment completely, because he'd felt that way once before. That time had long since passed. "You don't have to come in with me."

"No, no. I should. It's just…there's a part of me that knew exactly what she meant. I remember listening and understanding what she said at the time, because the same thing had happened to me."

He didn't say anything. He wasn't sure he could. Air felt trapped in his lungs. "Is that it?" he finally forced out. She didn't answer and kept her gaze straight ahead as she walked to Cobie's front door. Chris bounded after her. "Hey! Back up, Stark."

He stepped in front of her and rapped on the door—which swung open without resistance. His stomach plummeted. An open door was not a good sign.

"Miss Cobie May? This is Special Agent Barton of the FBI—"

"No!" Natasha shouted and rushed past him into the house. He grabbed her wrist as she crossed in front of him, stalling her from getting more than a few feet into the foyer—and then his eyes landed on what had sent her barreling through the door. The heel of a foot was visible through the living room doorway.

"Tasha, let me go first." She resisted for a moment, then let him lead. The last thing he needed was for her to step into another room rigged with a bomb, or come across another emotionally traumatic scene.

Too late, he thought as he crossed the threshold into the living room. *Once again we're too late. What happens if I'm too late to save Natasha next time?*

Cobie May lay facedown on her living room floor. Dark red liquid pooled around her upper body and head, and her limbs were splayed at awkward angles, indicating that she hadn't had a chance to break her fall. She'd been dead before she hit the floor.

Deep breaths. She needed to take deep, steady breaths so she could logically think her way through the situation. Emotion would cloud her judgment, and that wouldn't help either of them. To stay focused, she tried searching for anything out of place.

"There's no gun," she finally said. Her voice sounded strange to her own ears, but she held the words steady.

"What are you saying?"

She turned to see Chris in the doorway. "Where's the gun? I had one. Evans had one. Where's hers? It's not here."

Chris strode across the room to stand between her and the body, shielding the scene from view. "You should wait in the car."

"Chris, *where is it*?"

Chris pressed his lips together, brow furrowing. "Natasha. Listen to me. I'm going to look for it, but there's no guarantee there'll be one here. This looks different from what we saw with you and Dr. Evans."

That wasn't good enough. "Was she murdered?"

"I can't answer that right now."

"Stop it. I've been chased and shot at and now two of my fellow crew members are dead. I need to know. Do *you* think she was murdered?"

He ran his hand down his face, closing his eyes briefly as if to shut in the sadness—but she saw it, hovering at the edges. The events of the day were affecting him, too—and she found that comforting. He cared. He wouldn't allow injustice to go unpunished.

"Chris?"

"Don't quote me. This isn't an official supposition, but based on a cursory scan of the room, I highly doubt that Cobie May took her own life."

"Okay. All right." Her stomach flopped, over and over, like a colony of bats had taken roost in her insides and were now desperate to escape. She needed to remain calm, think this through. Who would harm Cobie May? Who would harm *any* of them?

"No, you're not okay." Chris placed his hands on either side of her face. "This isn't all right, and don't force yourself to pretend everything is fine. You just remembered how much you care about this woman, that you're friends, and now she's been taken away from you. You're allowed to be devastated."

She felt the corners of her mouth tug downward in response, but she refused to open the floodgates. "That could have been me. Should have been me, if yesterday morning is anything to go by. That's two down. Two people I care about gone forever, and it was almost three. My daughter…"

"I'm not going to let that happen to you. I promise."

The funny thing was, she believed him. She also wondered why, of all the things to be thinking about at a time like this, her brain had chosen to focus on the warmth of his fingertips against her skin. The closeness of his mouth to hers.

The way his thumb strayed toward the edge of her bottom lip.

And maybe she was imagining things, but she thought she saw the pull she felt toward him reflected in Chris's eyes. In the slight parting of his lips, in the way he leaned closer to her as they spoke.

Then Chris cleared his throat and pulled away from her, dispersing the undeniable static charge that had built in the air between them.

"I'm calling a team over. We need to mobilize as many resources as we can to get this figured out."

"Good plan." She released the breath she'd been holding and stepped back, blinking to find clarity. What had she been thinking? She hadn't, and that was the problem. She couldn't allow her thoughts to stray like that—talk about illogical, not to mention ill advised, especially without her memories of the events that had occurred in their past. She'd ask him about it soon, but there were more important things to deal with right now. "We need to contact the others, immediately. Get teams to them if we can't reach them by phone. They need to be warned before—"

The front window in the living room shattered.

Natasha screamed, and Chris yanked on her arm, pulling them both down to the floor. She hit the ground on her stomach, all the air forced from her lungs on impact. She gasped for air and curled into a ball, arms over her head as a hail of bullets peppered the living room. Couch stuffing burst from the cushions; mirrors and pictures on the wall broke into deadly shards as pieces of glass flew every which way like shrapnel. The bullets that didn't hit room fixtures thudded into the back wall of the living room—right where Chris's and Natasha's heads had been only moments ago.

"Who's shooting at us?" Natasha shouted over the noise, right before she heard it. Every nerve flared in alarm. *Something is buzzing.*

"It's the drone!" Chris called back. The buzz was loud enough to be heard over the sounds of gunfire, which meant the device was close. Right outside the window, in fact, and it had shattered the glass to get inside. "We have to move! It's going to fly into the house!"

As if on cue, the buzzing grew even louder

as the drone approached the shattered remains of the front windowpane.

Natasha could feel the driving of her pulse throughout her entire body, but for the first time since yesterday morning, she suddenly felt like she'd been granted a measure of clarity. They had an escape route; they only had to reach it in one piece. She pointed upward and mouthed, *Upstairs*. Changing their vertical orientation would give them a moment to find a hiding spot while the drone operator adjusted to follow them, rather than risk getting immediately shot in the back if they headed down the hall on the ground floor.

Chris nodded once, and that was all the time they had. Natasha used her core strength to spring to her feet. She beat Chris to the stairs, and their feet pounded up the staircase as hot lead decorated the walls and the railing behind them, demolishing photos that lined the walls.

Natasha had no idea which room would be the best to hide in, but since they didn't have time to debate the pros and cons, she chose the first open door and dived inside. Chris plunged in after her, slammed the door behind them and locked it.

Natasha's heart leaped into her throat as she took in the space. They were in a bathroom, a small, rectangular area with no real place to hide. It barely fit her and Chris comfortably. How would they dodge bullets in such a tiny area? Unless…

She glanced at Chris, and the moment they locked eyes, she knew they'd both come to the same conclusion. They climbed into the bathtub, then drew the curtain shut. The bathroom still had a window, but it was much smaller than any of the ones downstairs and—now that she thought of it—was likely smaller than the bedroom windows, too.

"You think that thing could come around the other side of the house and get in through this window?" she asked Chris.

"Not a chance," he said. He drew his weapon and backed up to the side of the tub nearest the door. "If it manages to break through this door and get inside, which I doubt, I can hit it from behind to hopefully take it down before it turns around and focuses on us. If it smashes the bathroom window, you stay low and I'll clip it from this angle. The window isn't wide enough for it to come inside, and it'll be difficult for the operator to get the correct downward angle into the tub to take a shot. By the time they get the weapon positioned, I'll have the drone incapacitated."

The confidence of his words filled Natasha with hope. They were going to get out of this alive. "Give me your phone so I can call the police."

"They're definitely on their way after all that noise," he said as he tossed his phone to her. "Make the call, but stay quiet. I think I hear it coming up the stairs."

Natasha strained to listen as she dialed 911. The low hum of the drone sounded. She hoped Chris was wrong and the drone operator had decided to leave them alone. Who would go through so much effort to take her out? And Cobie, too?

She clenched and unclenched her fists as the call connected, but the initial flood of anxiety of the moment had begun to wane and she'd started to breathe easier. She was confident in Chris's ability. He'd take care of it. There was no need to be afraid. Had God brought this man into her life as her protector for this exact reason?

"Here it comes," Chris said. "It's heading up the stairs."

Sure enough, as her call connected, the humming grew louder.

So did the sound of wailing police sirens.

Chris was right—the police were already on their way. But so was the drone.

Their lives might depend on which one reached them first.

SEVEN

"Get down as flat as you can," Chris urged Natasha. "Tell the operator where we are in the house and that there's a team arriving outside."

She slid to the bottom of the bathtub, one arm covering her head while she held the phone to her ear with the other. *Good.* He didn't need to worry about her while he did his job to protect them, and he shouldn't have been surprised by it. Astronauts lived through intense stress on the job every day, just like he did in the FBI. Maybe more for them, he thought, since a wrong move under pressure for an astronaut meant death.

Just one more thing about Natasha that surprised him and which was not at all like the woman he'd known twelve years ago. He admired, respected and even envied her grace under pressure. Had she truly changed, or would she be a different person once her memories returned? He dared to hope for the former.

Head out of the clouds, Barton. Chris felt a tightness inside his chest, and he took slow, deep breaths to remain focused. Survival depended on calm, decisive action. When the moment came, he had confidence that he could make an accurate shot and keep them safe—and truth be told, part of him hoped the drone would make it through the door so he *could* take it down. At least then the FBI could dismantle the machine and have a chance to figure out where it came from.

From outside, screeching brakes told Chris that help had arrived, but maybe not soon enough.

As if aware of the shrinking window of opportunity, bullets slammed into the wooden bathroom door, splintering its thin paneling and embedding in the wall over the bathroom sink. The bathroom mirror shattered, and Natasha flinched beside him, muffling her cries.

A heavy thud came from downstairs, followed by the thump of multiple pairs of boots tromping into the building. Help had arrived, but it came at a cost. The drone spun away, its shadow disappearing from the holes it had created in the door. Its mechanical buzz grew quieter as it flew deeper into the house, and just when Chris wondered if the police team had caught the device after all, the distant sound of a bang followed by more shattering glass told him that it had made its escape. Whoever operated that drone was a skilled pilot, indeed.

"It's gone," he muttered to Natasha. "But stay here. I'm going to make sure those are our boys."

He couldn't be too careful. What if the machine had broken a window just to make them think it had left the scene? Bringing Natasha into the open held too much risk. He climbed out of the tub and opened the bathroom door a crack as footsteps pounded up the stairs.

Three FBI agents in tactical gear and two police officers were making their way up to the second floor, weapons drawn as they scanned the area. "Special Agent Barton, FBI," he said as he exited the bathroom. Some of the tension in his shoulders momentarily abated at seeing the well-armored team. "I think the device took off through a window up here. You'd better send someone outside after it before it gets away."

As if on cue, another police officer ran halfway up the stairs, blurting his report. "It's headed west, but we lost sight of it almost immediately. We sent two guys in a squad car after it anyway, but whoever's flying that thing knows the area and understands the tactical advantages of evasive navigation."

Chris holstered his weapon and resisted the urge to pound his fist through a wall. He couldn't get mad at the men standing in front of him; they'd only been doing their jobs.

"Is it safe?" Natasha whispered at him through the open door.

"For now, yes." She came alongside him, and they waited while the response team checked the rest of the rooms. Once they'd been given the all clear, Chris led Natasha back downstairs. As they passed the living room, he sensed her stiffen beside him. Two of her colleagues gone in one morning. How much more could she take?

"This is a crisis," she said as they reached the front door. "The other two from my team, we need to get to them before the drone operator or whoever's giving orders to the operator does. If they haven't gotten to them already." Her voice cracked, and she stared at the phone in her hands. "And if whoever did this doesn't get me first. That thing could be hiding in the trees or behind a car, literally anywhere."

"Yes, that's possible, but I don't imagine the drone operator will be able to manage this much longer. Next time it makes an appearance, we'll take it down. I can almost guarantee that, now that the police have seen it with their own eyes and know what we're dealing with." When she didn't respond, Chris touched her elbow in what he hoped was a gesture of reassurance. "And hey, I'm going to make sure there are FBI teams dispatched to your coworkers' locations immediately. Do you have phone numbers for the other two in that file?"

"Yes. It's out in the car."

"Let's grab that and have you call them while the teams are on the way."

"The FBI isn't going to want to do that?"

Chris lowered his voice as they exited the house. He kept her close to him as they made their way to the vehicle. He'd tried to talk her anxieties down, but she wasn't wrong to postulate the theory that the drone might have doubled back to wait for her outside. They couldn't be too careful. "Yes, and they will. But the Brevard County FBI office's resources are going to be strained with these two incidents plus our regular caseload, at least until we get some backup from another county. Right now we have the advantage. You've got the numbers and addresses right in front of you."

Natasha didn't hesitate to grab the folder once she'd climbed into the Suburban. She'd already dialed the first number by the time Chris was buckled into his seat. He offered her what he hoped was an encouraging smile, but the gesture felt forced and tight across his face. Even with so many law-enforcement professionals around, it was hard to guarantee safety. Truth be told, they were safer inside the Suburban with its bulletproof glass than they were inside the house, but it seemed as though with every inch they gained on the situation, they fell another foot behind.

And he was fairly certain Natasha felt the same way, because her own smile looked tense and uncertain. He hoped that they were able to contact the others in time—he might have prayed and asked God for it, too, if he didn't feel increasingly as if the very God Natasha believed in seemed to have abandoned her at the time when she needed Him the most.

"Hello? Brett Ward? This is Natasha Stark." She exhaled in relief and leaned her head against the back of the seat. Chris observed her as she spoke to her fellow astronaut. Blatant hope painted her face as she and Ward exchanged greetings—this crew member was still alive.

But for how long?

"Has anyone from NASA been in contact with you at all?" Natasha bit down on the inside of her cheek, fearing that at any moment, the other shoe would drop. She'd hear gunfire or screams on Brett's end and they would have been too late to warn him. "If you're near any windows, get away from them immediately. I mean it."

On the other end of the line, Brett laughed as though she'd told a joke. "What's all this about, Stark? I heard you didn't show up for an appointment the other day. The police called me and a few of us came into work to brainstorm where you might be—"

"We can talk about that later." Natasha took a deep breath, then blurted out the warning. "Right now I need to know you're in a safe and secure area. Are you at home? There's an FBI team en route to your house, but if you're out elsewhere, drop what you're doing and head to the nearest police station or into work, where it's secure." She pressed her lips together to wait for his response. A stunned silence came through the other end, though she heard the sound of shoes scuffling over carpet. "Ward?"

"What is this about, Stark? You're not a vague kind of person, and I don't appreciate it if you're trying to scare me for no reason."

Natasha glanced at Chris. The volume on her phone was turned up all the way, so despite not having the call on speaker, he'd quite obviously heard every word. *Can I tell him?* she mouthed. Chris nodded.

"I wish there was a better way to say this, that I could tell you in person, but here it is. Evans and May are dead. I saw their bodies. Evans looks like a suicide. May looks like a murder."

"What? Murder? Suicide? Cut it out, Stark. That's not funny."

"I would never make a joke like that, Ward. They're dead, and I've been attacked, and whoever did it is probably coming for you and Coulson next. They're still after me, too. I'm working with an FBI agent to make sense of what's happening. Where are you? There are FBI teams looking for both you and Coulson." She glanced at Chris, sudden panic rising in her throat. Despite not fully remembering these people, somewhere deep inside, she knew that she cared about them—that she'd give almost anything to keep them safe.

Ward cleared his throat, and when he spoke, he sounded shaken. "I'm at Kennedy. I came in a few hours ago to get some work done on our reports. I had a media interview, too, which May was supposed to be here for. I figured she'd gotten wrapped up in something at home and asked the reporter if we could reschedule. I had no idea… They're dead? Both of them?"

"Yes. I need to warn Coulson, so stay where you are, all right? All of those security upgrades they did before our mission makes NASA property one of the most secure areas around, even more than the police station. Settle in, okay?"

"What about you?" His voice hitched with emotion. "Are you all right?"

She sighed, unable to stop herself. "I'm fine. Mostly. Like I said, I'm with an FBI agent who's looking out for me." Her gaze slid over to Chris, who offered up a strained, one-sided smile. Despite the grimace, the kindness in his eyes was sincere. He looked so tense, so concerned, that she couldn't help herself—she reached over, grabbed his forearm and squeezed. His eyebrows nearly leaped off his face in surprise, so she pulled her hand away.

Her cheeks stung with the heat of embarrassment. Why had she done that?

"Mostly? What aren't you telling me?" Ward's voice sounded far off, like he stood in a large room without sound dampening—a gymnasium? Cafeteria? Natasha's hand tingled with warmth where she'd touched Chris's arm, and she balled her hand into a fist. He didn't need her comfort; he was a seasoned FBI agent. And he probably didn't *want* her comfort, if the hints he'd dropped about their unspoken past were anything to go by.

"I… Look, I guess I might as well tell you, so you don't think I've gone crazy if I say something stupid. Something did happen to me yesterday, and we'll talk about it later, but as a result I have psychogenic and retrograde amnesia. So, no, I'm not okay, but I will be. I really have to go." She pulled the phone away, ready to end the call.

"If we're all in danger, why aren't you here with me?" Ward's voice came through.

That made her pause. She pulled the phone back to her ear as she glanced at Chris with a shrug. "I'm being protected by an FBI agent. I'm in good hands."

"Doesn't sound like it. You've been at the scene of two deaths, and you're telling me to get away from open windows? I don't care who you're with, Stark—if you're out in the open, you're vulnerable. Come in to Kennedy with me. Like you said, it's safe here. Plus, we can be together."

"Be…together?" That was an odd way to phrase things. "I guess there's safety in numbers. I'll try to pull Coulson in, too."

"No. *Together.*"

"I don't understand."

"Together, you and me." Ward sounded incredulous. "Don't tell me that you don't remember. Natasha, we're not just coworkers."

A hot rush of anxiety washed over her as he used her first name. It sounded so personal, so much more intimate than when he'd called her by her last name. *Not just coworkers?* She hoped that he didn't mean what she thought he did—and then she wondered why she'd hope such a thing at all. "I don't understand."

"How could you forget? Never mind—it's fine. You've been through something traumatic. But you should come in, Natasha. We belong together, you and I. Let me keep you safe, the way I always have."

The phone dropped from Natasha's fingers.

EIGHT

Chris caught the phone as it fell, then pulled it to his ear. "This is Special Agent Chris Barton of the FBI. Mr. Ward, I advise you remain where you are at Kennedy and do not leave until we notify you that it's safe to do so. Until then, I'll be responsible for Ms. Stark's safety." He hung up and handed the phone back to Natasha. Her cheeks had paled, and her shoulders crept closer to her ears. "Are you all right? We need to contact Coulson. A team should be close to her house by now, but if you're not in the right head space to call her, I'll do it."

He reached for the folder on her lap, but she slammed her hands down on the top. "No, I'm okay. I'll do it. I just… I didn't expect that is all. I don't remember. Romantic entanglement at work? I know I don't have all my memories, but…that doesn't sound like me. That doesn't feel like me. I felt nothing when I spoke to him, but I remembered Hayley right away. I love her with every fiber of my being, and he made it sound as though— Never mind. I'm phoning Coulson."

Chris observed her movements as she dialed Coulson. Part of him wanted to tell her that it would be all right, that her feelings would return when her memories did, but another part of him fought the surprising flare of a green monster that threatened to push the wrong words out of his mouth. He didn't want her to be romantically involved with anyone else, but what right did he have to feel that way? Why couldn't he push away the emotions that kept bubbling to the surface? As soon as her memories returned, she'd want him as far away from her as possible, and he didn't want to be around someone who viewed her fellow humans on a sliding scale of value according to their socioeconomic status. But that was the Natasha he'd known in the past. He hadn't sensed any of that from her since the amnesia hit, but couldn't the loss of a person's memory also affect their personality to a degree? Maybe she'd forgotten about her prejudices along with everything else.

And her home...it had been so modest, not

to mention the astonishing kindness she'd done her neighbors by willingly giving up a larger condo unit so they'd have space for their new baby.

It didn't make sense—reconciling these two incarnations of Natasha Stark made his brain hurt. Regardless of which version of her was the true woman, it was also only natural that she'd have someone else in her life. Especially someone she'd worked closely with for so long. It happened all the time in law enforcement, partners falling in love and causing complications. Why would he have even entertained the notion that she'd be unattached twelve years later?

And yet while in her house yesterday he'd noted that she didn't have any photographs up on the fridge or on the walls of anyone except for herself and Hayley. Surely if she was deeply involved with someone, there'd be a few pictures around…unless she was protecting her daughter, keeping it quiet until the relationship was a sure thing. Her daughter, who might be *his* daughter. He shook his head, rubbing his eyes.

Why was he giving these thoughts head space right now? He needed to stop thinking about this and focus on the case. Her relationship status wasn't relevant to him. It didn't matter. All that mattered was her safety and the safety of the others on her crew.

Still, he couldn't help but wonder why she'd been wearing that gold name bracelet yesterday he'd given her so many years ago.

"Coulson didn't answer," Natasha said, pulling the phone away to punch in another number. "I left a message, but she's not there. I'm phoning HR for her schedule. The months before and after launch are so rigidly scheduled by NASA that they tend to know where we are down to the minute. If she's not on the schedule to be home today, they'll tell us where she is."

Chris started up the Suburban while she called in. He pulled out of the driveway and headed back toward the center of town so that they'd be on the move once they received directions. Besides, he needed to keep moving. His limbs and brain felt restless without motion—there was a killer on the loose, and the woman beside him remained a target.

After a brief conversation with the person on the other end of the line, Natasha hung up and tapped the phone against her hand. "You're not going to believe this. Coulson is on a speaking tour of local schools this week. She has two schools to speak at today."

"Nothing unusual about that," Chris said. "What's the part I'm not going to believe? Which school is she visiting right now? We should get a team over there right away. I want to think that she'd be safe in a public school around children, but if there's one thing I've learned on this job, it's never to underestimate your opponent. Where is she?"

Natasha's voice cracked as she spoke. "She's at Hayley's school, Chris. She's at the middle school for a twelve-thirty assembly. I don't want my daughter anywhere near astronauts right now. None of us are safe. I want her moved to NASA property for the rest of the day."

"Don't schools have some solid security of their own these days? But I can certainly ask the officer on duty at the school to take her over, or see if there are FBI teams closer than us who can move her and Coulson."

He reached to the center console and activated the Bluetooth system, but Natasha's hand landed on his. A shiver ran up his arm and down his spine at her touch, despite the urgency.

"Chris, call backup if you want, but according to the phone's GPS, we're literally three minutes from the school. We'll be there before a team even gets mobilized. The one that went to Coulson's house is likely six or seven minutes away."

He agreed with her. This was a matter of life and death, and if they could make it to the school first and potentially save Coulson's life, they needed to do it. "All right, we're going. But when we get there, you need to stay close."

"You think there'd be an attack on Coulson at the school? Chris, there are hundreds of kids at that school. My daughter—"

"We're going to get Coulson out, get a team to pull Hayley and remove any potential risk to the school."

"Another team for my daughter? Shouldn't she come with us?"

"You just said that you don't want her anywhere near astronauts, and I agree. You and Coulson are still potential targets, so it will be safer for the two of you and Hayley to travel separately just in case. We'll get you moved quickly and reunited once you're secure on NASA property. Everything is going to be all right." He had to believe that.

Less than three minutes later, Chris slammed the Suburban into Park at the front of the school. The familiar ring of sirens in the distance told him that backup was on the way, but he hoped with every fiber of his being that it wasn't needed aside from the team that would escort Hayley in a separate vehicle. Natasha led the way to the main office. Chris flashed his badge as they rushed into the room.

"Chris Barton, FBI. We have reason to believe that your guest speaker is in danger. Where is she?"

The receptionist leaped out of her seat in alarm, mouth agape. "I don't… The gym! The students are gathered for a special holiday assembly, but—"

"Which direction?"

"Down the hall to your left, then take another right—"

"Lead the way, please," Natasha said, gesturing to the door. The receptionist stood frozen in alarm. *"Now."*

The woman scurried out the office door and down the festively decorated hall, Chris and Natasha close on her heels. Chris dared to hope that they'd finally managed to get one step ahead of their foe. The receptionist's surprise was actually a good sign.

"Right here," the receptionist exclaimed, pointing to a set of swinging double doors covered with red-and-green wrapping paper. Square windows in the upper half of each door were framed with silver ribbon and shiny red bows. Chris didn't bother to look through the windows—he pushed through the doors and marched to the nearest teacher, a white-haired fellow in a reindeer sweater. The man stumbled backward in surprise as Chris flashed his badge and introduced himself.

"I'm going to have to ask you to evacuate this gymnasium and place the school on lockdown," he said to the startled teacher. Several others stepped forward to listen as he kept his voice low to deliver instructions. "Your guest speaker may be in danger. I'm going to escort her to safety, but the longer she's around these children, the greater the risk becomes that they'll be caught in any potential cross fire. Please return the students to their classrooms and keep them calm. Whatever your emergency protocol is for an attacker inside the school, make it happen. FBI backup is on the way to assist and to remove Hayley Stark from the premises, but no one else is to leave until you get the all clear. We'll let you know when it's safe."

The teachers began asking questions and demanding more information, but Chris had no intention of offering up anything more just yet—he was more concerned with the stern-looking, short-haired woman on the podium. She stood behind a man in a Santa hat who had the demeanor of a school principal. The man looked over and caught Chris's eye, then noticed the commotion of teachers near the gym doors. The principal excused himself and asked the students to hold tight for a moment, then headed toward them.

"Let's go," Chris said to Natasha. They proceeded toward the podium. When Melinda Coulson turned to see what had stopped the principal in the middle of his introduction, she frowned, eyes blinking rapidly in confusion.

"Stark? What are you doing here?" She marched toward them as one of the teachers announced to the students that they were to follow their teachers back to their classrooms. Groans and whines erupted throughout the gym, but Chris tried to stay focused.

"Melinda Coulson, I'm FBI Special Agent Chris Barton, and we have reason to believe you're in danger," he said.

Coulson raised an eyebrow at him, then turned to Natasha. "Stark? What is he talking about? Does this have anything to do with your disappearance? I got a phone call from

Wanda in HR yesterday asking if I'd seen or heard from you."

"Yes and no, but I'll explain that later. He's telling the truth—you and I are in danger."

"All right, but can you tell me more of what this is about? Why are the children being evacuated?"

"It's Evans and May," Natasha said. Her voice had gone flat and toneless, shifting once again to work mode to detach her emotions from reality. Chris wanted to reassure her that it was all right to be upset, that she and her coworker could take a moment together if needed, but she was observing the sea of students as they moved, her eyes trained on one in particular. Chris's mouth grew dry as he made the connection. Hayley followed her class, heading out of the gym. She waved at her mom, and Natasha waved back, offering a reassuring smile to her daughter—maybe *his* daughter, too—that contrasted with the finality of her next words to Coulson. "They're dead."

Coulson's lips parted, and she stared at Natasha, processing her words. "They're...what?"

"Let's go now, please." Chris needed to hustle the two women to safety in the Suburban. The sooner they left the school, the better. The teachers were doing an excellent job of herding the children back to their classrooms in an orderly fashion. Despite the fear in the adults' eyes, they kept their voices calm and reassured the students as Chris, Natasha and Coulson passed by. He heard more than one excited gasp as some of the students recognized there were now two astronauts in their midst. Chris's stomach twisted, seeing the wide-eyed adoration of these young girls and boys. Stark and Coulson were their heroes, people that these kids looked up to and aspired to become when they grew up. What would happen to their innocent optimism, their big dreams, if anything happened to these women? The children would be shattered, even more than they already would be when Titusville and the rest of the country learned about the deaths of Evans and May. The community was already going to have a hard time dealing with the loss at what should be a joyous time of year. It would be a somber Christmas for some of Titusville's families, and Chris would do everything in his power to make sure that no one else spent their Christmas in mourning instead of joy.

Chris nodded to the principal as they passed, grateful for the staff's decisive action. As they reached the front doors of the school, Chris paused to survey the sky. There was deeper cloud cover now than there'd been a few hours ago, and the humidity in the air suggested an impending rain shower. He didn't like the idea of a drone being able to hide in the low clouds, but he and the others couldn't remain inside the school. At least he'd had the foresight to pull the Suburban up as close as he could to the front doors, so they didn't have far to go to get inside the vehicle and behind its bulletproof glass. If Natasha and Coulson crouched down behind the front seats, they'd be even smaller targets.

"Is it safe?" Natasha joined him, her gaze whipping back and forth. "Can we make it?"

"I don't see or hear it," he said. "But that doesn't mean it's not there."

Coulson cleared her throat behind them. "Excuse me? What's not there?"

"Attack drone," Natasha said. Chris looked at her sharply. "What? It's not like she wasn't going to find out if it dropped out of the sky and started firing. I'd say this goes beyond need-to-know information."

She was right. He drew his weapon and opened the front door, using his foot to brace the door in place. "I'm going to move out in front of you and provide cover in case the drone appears. Coulson, get inside the vehicle and make yourself as small a target as possible. Natasha, go with her. I'll be right behind you."

"Where are you taking us?" Coulson sounded incredulous, but she recovered quickly, her tone shifting to the matter-of-fact practicality he recognized from these past few days spent with Natasha. "How did Evans and May die? Are you sure they're gone?"

Despite her tone, she couldn't bury all her emotion. The fear and disbelief in her eyes gave her away, and he wished there was more time to explain. Natasha could speak to her coworker later, when they were safe and secure. Chris stepped outside, weapon in hand, and scanned their surroundings. There was no sign of the drone. He unlocked the SUV with the key fob and waved the women forward. They ran out of the building without hesitation, staying low as Natasha ushered her colleague ahead of her. Coulson climbed into the vehicle, and Natasha stepped up after her. Chris dared to harbor a shred of hope that they'd managed to save Coulson's life, when he heard shouting from inside the school.

Natasha paused, one foot up on the Suburban's runner. Chris gestured for her to get inside, but instead she shut Coulson's door and ran back toward the school. The shouting became clearer as she passed him.

"Ms. Stark? Ms. Stark!" The receptionist appeared in the doorway. "Just double-checking—you're taking Hayley home for the rest of the day?"

A chill ran down Chris's spine. What would make her ask a question like that? He glanced at Natasha, whose steps had slowed. Her breathing had deepened, as though she was fighting hard to remain calm.

"What? No, there's a separate FBI team coming for her. Traveling with us is a safety risk."

The receptionist looked over her shoulder into the school, then back at Natasha and past her to the Suburban. "She's not in the vehicle with you? She didn't go with you just now?"

"No," Natasha said. "It's safer for her to remain here until her FBI escort arrives. Why? Where is she?" When the receptionist didn't respond, Chris placed his hand on Natasha's shoulder for support as her tone grew louder and sharper. "Where's my daughter?"

"Hayley's teacher assumed she was with you." The receptionist glanced between them, pressing her palms together.

"What are you saying?" Natasha's stomach plummeted into her shoes. A tingling sensation began to worm its way up her spine, and her limbs grew cold even as sweat broke out across her forehead. "She's not with me. So where is she?"

Beside her, the beep of Chris locking the Suburban was followed by a tug on her arm. She didn't resist as Chris pulled her back inside the safety of the school and holstered his weapon. "Where is Hayley Stark?" he growled.

The receptionist's mouth hung open as she shook her head. Her complexion grew pale as Natasha stepped closer.

"There has to be a logical explanation for this," Chris said, but she suspected he was thinking the same thing as her—it could be no coincidence that of all the students in the entire school, Natasha's daughter was the one who'd disappeared. "Did you check the bathrooms? The office? Other classrooms?"

"One of the teachers checked the restroom next to her class, but she wasn't there. That's when Ms. Jakes thought maybe she'd left with you."

Chris gripped Natasha's upper arms and drew her toward him so that she faced him. She tried to stop the trembling—it wasn't useful, wasn't a logical response to help solve the problem—but her body rebelled as fear for her daughter took a fast and firm hold.

He met her eyes and she saw determination. He would help her. He'd find Hayley, and everything would be okay. "Would she have attempted to walk home? Do you have a safety plan for emergencies that she'd have decided to follow?"

"I don't know—I don't know." Natasha shook her head as her eyes began to burn with tears. She blinked them away before they could fall. "I don't remember. I'm trying, but I don't remember."

"Search the school," Chris told the receptionist. "Get everyone on it who can be spared and start looking for the girl. I'll have the FBI send someone to her home and use the most logical route in case she decided to walk or bus back. We're going to find her, Natasha."

She blinked without agreement. A single tear escaped from the corner of her eye and rolled down her cheek, though her jaw remained set. How could she help her daughter if she became an emotional mess? "I need her, Chris. She's my everything. She's the only family I have."

Strictly speaking, she knew that wasn't true.

But memories of her parents were blurry and the flashes she had of her father were not positive. They'd had…a falling-out. A disagreement? Something bad had happened, and it was locked away inside her head with everything else.

Another tear threatened to escape, but Chris gently brushed his thumb underneath her eye, wiping it away before it fell. As he pulled his hand back, Natasha sensed a shift between them. Something had just happened, but she didn't know what.

He cleared his throat and crossed his arms. "We'll find her and keep her safe. I'm sure this is all a big misunderstanding."

The moment evaporated like smoke. How could he honestly say those words to her after everything she'd gone through so far? Two of her coworkers dead in one day and now her daughter was missing. How could that be a misunderstanding? During mission training at NASA, astronauts prepared for every eventuality by running simulations for each potential incident—even their own deaths—but she'd never anticipated a situation like this. What she wouldn't give to work out this scenario in a room somewhere first.

Tires squealed outside as police cars and FBI

vehicles pulled into the parking lot, sirens blaring to announce their arrival.

Three news vans also pulled into the lot behind them. Natasha supposed it was inevitable that word would get out to the media eventually, but part of her had hoped they'd have more time to deal with the situation before the deaths and attacks got plastered across television and radio broadcasts. Her first priority was finding Hayley. "Has anyone searched the outside grounds? The playground area, the bushes? Maybe she took off with a friend to spend time outdoors. She's not the kind of kid to up and disappear." Natasha's cheeks warmed under Chris's scrutiny. "She's not. I know, give it another year or so, but she only just turned twelve. The rebellion and angst haven't kicked in yet."

"That's fine, but you're not searching out there in the open. There are enough people here to handle it. It'll be safer for you to wait in the car with Coulson until this gets sorted out."

"And if it doesn't? My daughter is missing. I have every right to help find her."

"No, you don't." Chris dropped his hands to his hips. "I understand you want to help find her, but how much good will you be to her if there's another open attack? What happens when one of those bullets finds its mark? You've evaded serious injury so far, but I can't in good conscience continue to put you in a position where more shots can be fired in your direction. Drone, human, I don't care where it comes from, I don't want you making yourself a target."

She understood his words, but logic didn't always outweigh a mother's instinct to protect her child. "Agent Barton, do you have any children?" He flinched, a flicker of panic crossing his face. Had she imagined it? "I'm sorry—but I need you to understand where I'm coming from."

"No, it's fine. I get it." His nod was terse, and he refused to meet her eyes. How strange. What did she know about him, anyway? She hadn't asked before now, and it hadn't come up. For all she knew, she could be dredging up a painful memory. "Let's get you into the Suburban," he grunted. He pushed through the front doors of the school as they were approached by several pairs of officers—it looked like two FBI agents and two local police officers. Chris nodded at each of them in acknowledgment as he stepped outside and gestured for Natasha to follow. "We'll have teams searching inside and out, understand? As of this moment, we're mobilizing to do everything we can to protect your family, as well as Coulson and Ward. The last thing anyone wants is for this to turn into a national incident where the media's prying eyes point to you as you're trying to grieve the loss of your crew members. I know you think you can handle this with all that fancy NASA problem-solving training that's been keeping you calm, but you can't stay a robot forever. You'll have to let yourself feel, sooner or later, and..." The sharp tone slid from his voice, and his gaze took on a surprising softness. "I won't let your family turn into a national sob story. You know the media will eat up the amnesia angle if the news gets out. The longer we can keep you out of the spotlight, the better for you and Hayley."

He made an excellent point, but as they reached the Suburban, the roar of another powerful engine cut through the crackles and clicks of police radio chatter coming from the assortment of vehicles in the school lot. A burgundy Range Rover careened down the street next to the school and veered into the parking lot with the screech of balding, overworked tires. Chris's hands reached for his sidearm, but a thumping sound from inside Chris's vehicle snagged Natasha's attention.

Melinda Coulson pounded on the window, her form barely visible through the tinted glass. Natasha tapped Chris and pointed, and he quickly unlocked the Suburban. Coulson tumbled out with a look of relief on her face and a cell phone in her hand.

"Ward's here," she said. "He came to pick us up."

"Pick us up?" Natasha glanced at Chris and back at Coulson. "I'm not going anywhere until Hayley is found."

"Hayley's missing? What happened?" Natasha didn't trust herself to speak, so she said nothing. Coulson's face fell. "I'm so sorry. She waved hi to me when I arrived for the assembly."

"You'll have time to discuss the details later," Chris growled as the burgundy Range Rover blasted past the officers and vehicles trying to wave it down. They jumped out of the way before they got smoked by the driver, and there was no mistaking the anger in Chris's expression as the vehicle screeched while it parked next to his Suburban. The driver's door swung open and the man that Natasha recognized from the astronaut personnel files as Brett Ward practically sprinted the three yards to her side—but he didn't stop there. Natasha coughed in surprise as Ward threw his arms around her and pulled her to his chest, pressing her head against his shoulder. She tucked her arms between them and gently pushed him away, uncomfortable with the gesture. He held on a moment longer than necessary before taking her not-so-subtle hint, releasing her and stepping back. She heard a sharp intake of breath from Coulson on her right.

"You shouldn't be here," Natasha said. "Why did you leave Kennedy? Chris told you to stay at NASA, where it's safe."

"Chris?" Ward frowned. "Who?"

Natasha sensed a flush creeping up her neck. "Agent Barton."

Ward swung his gaze between herself, Coulson and Chris. "Melinda called me and said you'd escorted her out of the school."

"I didn't know you'd already talked to him," Coulson said apologetically. "But now that we're all here, can we help search for Hayley?"

"Search for Hayley? What's going on?" Ward inched forward as if to wrap his arms around Natasha again, but she held up a hand to stop him. "Seriously? What's going on with you today?"

"What's going on with the two of you at all," Coulson muttered. Natasha filed away her coworker's disbelief. It gave weight to the uneasy feeling she had about Ward, but his physical gestures seemed genuine. She had no doubt he cared about her. So why didn't she feel anything toward him? She couldn't muster even an inkling of affection.

Chris broke away from the FBI agent who'd approached him to speak about the situation and slid into their group huddle. "All of you, get in the Suburban right now. Ward, I don't know what you're doing here, but you're now the responsibility of the FBI, so get in the car. We'll talk about your reckless driving charges later. It won't be taken lightly. You could have killed someone."

"Incoming at three o'clock!" shouted a nearby officer. "Barton, this your bird?"

Chris scowled at the three of them, and Natasha's heart crumpled at his show of anger. She wanted to apologize and explain that she truly didn't remember being in a relationship with Ward, but she also knew deep in her heart that Ward wasn't the issue here. Why would Chris be upset about any of Natasha's relationships? And what made her think she needed to apologize to Chris? They weren't involved. Her relationships weren't any of his business. It made no sense, and it meant her brain was reading into things that weren't even there instead of focusing on the immediate danger.

"Into the vehicle," Chris ordered. "All of you." He turned away from them and drew his weapon. Natasha hesitated to leave his side, but as the first shot rang out from the incoming drone, followed by gunfire from law enforcement trying to bring it down, reality sank in and she dived for the safety of the reinforced Suburban.

Coulson climbed in first. Bullets whipped by over their heads as Natasha got in after her, followed by Ward. She suppressed a scream at the metallic thud of heated lead embedding into the door as Ward yanked it shut.

"Go, go, go!" They heard Chris shout instructions to the others outside. "It's circling—stay alert!"

In the relative safety of the vehicle, seated between two crew members whom she barely remembered but should have known well, the weight of Hayley's disappearance crashed down around her.

She buried her face in her hands, listening to the shouts and noises outside. Each passing second sent another bullet slamming into the Suburban, and the echoing report of the police and FBI's shots in response only served to drive home the point: if *she* wasn't safe, if someone was trying to get to her and hadn't succeeded by other means thus far, they'd probably taken Hayley. Every moment without her daughter increased the possibility that Hayley wouldn't be found alive.

An arm dropped across her shoulders as three bullets hit the windshield, sending spiderweb cracks across the glass. How much longer would it hold?

"They'll find her," Coulson murmured. "These guys are good. The media being here is a good thing. It means word will spread and whoever has done this will have a harder time hiding."

"Drone's gone," said Ward after several seconds of sudden silence. He threw open the Suburban's door without waiting for an all clear from the FBI and hopped out of the car.

"What do you think you're doing?" Chris rushed to the vehicle, his weapon still drawn. "The threat hasn't been neutralized. It's still out here somewhere. Get back inside."

"I think it's pretty clear that your guys don't know how to handle this," Ward said, glancing back at Natasha as if expecting her to agree with him. Clearly he didn't know her as well as he thought he did. "We're heading back to

Kennedy while you search for Stark's daughter. Sitting here and getting shot at isn't helping anyone, and you know as well as I do that bulletproof glass can only take so many hits. I'm trained to think in contingencies. What happens if another drone comes screaming through the air toward us?"

Chris's scowl eased up. Natasha saw the reluctance on his face to agree with Ward, but the man made some good points.

"You can't protect her here," Ward spit. "You want to keep her out of danger? You're doing a terrible job. She's coming with me."

Natasha swallowed hard on the lump forming in her throat. Did she even want to go with Ward? Chris had been doing everything as best he could, playing by the book and following orders from the FBI. She hadn't once felt that he was shirking his duty by keeping her with him, and she was only still with him due to her own insistence on helping out. Ward spoke the truth—the attacks kept coming, and sooner or later, even bulletproof glass wouldn't keep her or her fellow astronauts safe. And Chris had said himself that if things got dicey, he'd take her to NASA property for safe harbor.

She met Chris's eyes and, to her great surprise, saw a flicker of buried pain push to the surface. He didn't want to let her go; she saw it clear as day.

And even more surprising, she didn't want to leave his side, either.

"Go," he said, his words so contrary to what she read on his face that it took a moment for her brain to process the connection. "Go with Ward. He's right—at this point, staying with me is going to get you killed."

Of course he wanted her to leave. She was a liability, another body to get in the way while he tried to do his job. And if he had the freedom and space to do his job, he'd find Hayley.

She blinked away more tears, banishing them as she spoke her next words. Her voice sounded so thin and strained to her own ears that she wasn't sure he'd hear it above the din in the parking lot. "Find my daughter, Chris. Please. You know best what's been going on. I know you can."

He heard her. He cupped her cheek and spoke with authority. "I'll find her. I promise. Now go!"

NINE

The words felt like nails pulled one at a time from his mouth. He didn't want to tell her to leave, didn't want to tell her to turn around and go someplace else where he couldn't personally be certain that she was safe and secure.

But the truth of the matter was, if Ward took Natasha back to NASA, he *could* be certain of all those things. He'd seen the place himself, and it was locked down better than most government buildings he'd visited since joining the FBI.

What he hadn't counted on when he said those words, however, was the look of utter betrayal on Natasha's face. He wanted to explain, use logic that she'd understand—but they had no time to stand around and talk it out. The drone reappeared from behind a parked vehicle and swooped lower, but its attempts to take shots at the SUV and the astronauts were becoming less accurate as each dip and spin took on a frantic edge. Gunfire from the local police clipped the sides of the drone's rotating blades, sending it flipping end over end, whirling sideways through the air.

Someone needed to get a clean shot at its front—and especially at the camera undoubtedly mounted at the front of the device in order to allow its controller to maneuver with ease and fire with near-deadly accuracy.

"Chris?"

He risked a glance at Natasha, who was being ushered away to Ward's vehicle with Coulson close behind. He wanted to run to her and explain that this was a last resort, that his heart and conscience couldn't allow her to remain in the line of fire. Her body *and* mental state were at significant risk, and remaining with her crew was the best option. On the other hand, her temporal amnesia had taken away that familiarity and knowledge of Ward and Coulson—so did that mean he'd just sent her into an even more difficult and mentally taxing situation?

He waved over another nearby FBI agent. The man sidestepped to Chris's side, keeping one eye on the drone as he moved.

"See that Range Rover?" Chris asked the agent, who nodded the affirmative. "We have three national assets inside that vehicle. They're heading back to NASA's secured facility at Kennedy, where they can go on lockdown until Hayley Stark is found and we have this situation resolved. I need you to lead an FBI escort to ensure they reach the place without hazard. There have already been two episodes on the road involving Natasha Stark, and on both occasions the vehicle fled as soon as law enforcement arrived on the scene in active pursuit. Keeping an FBI vehicle close to them will ensure there are officers at the ready in the event of another incident. Take someone with you."

The agent took off at Chris's dismissal, grabbing his nearest fellow agent to go with him. Chris watched closely as the team climbed into their FBI-issue Suburban and pulled out close behind Ward's Range Rover. An uneasy feeling settled in Chris's gut as he watched the two vehicles drive away, but he couldn't pinpoint exactly why or where it came from. He was doing the right thing. All evidence of the past few days pointed to this being the correct course of action. Why wouldn't he send the astronauts to a secure location where no one could get to them, including the drone?

It just made sense, and having law enforcement keep an eye on them for the duration of the drive was an extra precaution. He'd have preferred to go with them and keep Natasha in his sights the entire time, but knowing that he was on the case to find Hayley would give her peace of mind. Plus, he'd been the one sitting at the front of the attacks with Natasha, which she'd pointed out. That did make him better equipped than anyone else to lead the search for her daughter.

Their daughter. Even though they hadn't been able to discuss it yet, Chris was certain—beyond certain—that Hayley was his daughter. If anything happened to her before he heard the truth from Natasha herself, before he'd had a chance to get to know Hayley, he would never, ever forgive himself. Failure was not an option. He needed to keep Hayley alive, and the best chance he had of that was to locate her as fast as possible.

A vise tightened around his insides as he thought of his little girl being forcibly taken from the school. How had no one heard her scream for help? A twelve-year-old would be strong enough to put up a decent fight, and in a school full of students and teachers, surely that wouldn't go unnoticed.

A stranger in the school…that would have tipped off the security staff on duty, too, wouldn't it? Schools were secure these days, with extra measures to keep students and staff safe, so it wasn't as if a total stranger could have waltzed through the halls, knocked out a preteen to avoid the struggle of resistance and then walked out the door with her slung over his or her shoulder.

That left one other really viable option: Hayley knew her abductor.

The second possible explanation was that the girl had decided to leave school on her own and was on her way home, but officers had been sent to check those potential routes first, and no one had called to tell him otherwise.

In this case, no news was not good news by any stretch.

The loud buzzing of the drone pulled Chris's focus back to the danger of the present. The device wobbled in the air as it flew straight toward him. It fired, but the shot went wide as he slipped behind the bumper of his Suburban. In a crouch, he took a deep breath, steadying his adrenaline-fueled limbs and finding the center of calm he'd need to bring a finish to this ridiculous drone situation that refused to end.

He closed his eyes and listened as it came

nearer, shutting out his other senses until it was just him and the sound of the machine. He needed it to come closer. As close as possible. He'd get one chance, one shot at this range, and he had to make it count—and do it quickly, before the operator on the other end shot first. Chris had a plan, and the longer it took to execute, the more time they lost to search for Hayley.

Whether you're my little girl or not, I'm going to bring you home, he silently promised. *There will be no more tears for your mom this Christmas.*

His eyes snapped open as the buzzing grew just…loud…enough.

With singular focus and impeccable aim, Chris stood, aimed for the thin black strip at the front of the device and exhaled. The drone hovered less than five feet away.

He fired.

A second bang split the air as the drone lurched backward, spinning like a flipped coin and flying end over end as though tossed. Its buzzing petered off to a high-pitched whine. It lost momentum and slammed into the ground. Pieces of metal and plastic splintered and skittered across the school sidewalk.

Half the FBI agents and police officers ran

for the device, but Chris reached it first. He spun the machine so that its mounted firearm pointed away from the school and his people, then grabbed on to it and wrenched with all his might.

The firearm's mount bent and snapped with a satisfying crack. He dropped the gun into an evidence bag and handed it to another agent so she could pass it off to the FBI's Evidence Response team once they arrived. If everything went well, one of the FBI's tech teams might be able to hack into the device and figure out where it had originated from—perhaps reverse-locate the IP to learn who had been controlling it. He doubted it would be that easy, but he wouldn't toss away hope just yet.

After all that he and Natasha had gone through, it felt a little anticlimactic to see the device lying there, nothing but a pile of broken machinery. How had this lifeless device caused so much fear and done so much damage? He'd be happy to see the operator behind bars—and even happier to call Natasha and let her know that this threat against her life, at least, had ended.

Unless the operator had another drone.

No, he couldn't think like that. This drone looked like serious, expensive tech—military grade, he might even venture—not the kind of thing an everyday civilian could afford.

He wouldn't rule it out, to be safe, but he also needed to focus on finding Hayley as quickly as possible.

A sensation of uncertainty wove its way through his insides, battling against nausea as he racked his brain for ideas concerning Hayley's location. He thought he might check in and around Natasha's home himself, see if it jogged any other clues. Did Natasha know where her neighbors had holed themselves up while their condo was being rebuilt? Maybe Hayley had taken off to stay with the neighbors as part of a misguided attempt to follow safety protocol.

Chris pulled out his phone to call Natasha and ask for her neighbor's cell number when the device lit up and buzzed in his hand. The caller ID remained blank, but he had a good idea what that meant. His boss was calling.

"Barton," he answered.

"Barton? Good. Listen, we got a rush on ballistics for the Stark case. You're going to want to act quickly on this before the press grabs it and eats us alive. You at the middle school in town?"

"Yes, sir." There was a twisting in Chris's

gut at the sound of his boss's voice. To be personally called by the officer in charge in the middle of a case that he'd been independently working on these past few days was *not* a good sign. "We've clipped the bird's wings and the device is being examined and cleaned up by Evidence Response. I'll have it sent back to the office so that tech can get their hands on it and try to figure out where it came from."

"Great, great, but listen—let the other boys handle it. You need to make an arrest, and it's not going to be pretty. I called you personally because of your history on this."

Chris's mouth grew dry. "What's going on, sir? What did ballistics say?"

"The gun in Stark's possession when you found her," said the officer in charge, "is a ballistics and residue match for the bullet that killed Cobie May. I'm sorry, but your so-called victim is now a murder suspect."

Natasha stared out the window as Ward drove her and Coulson through the town toward the safety of Kennedy Space Center, the radio blaring peppy Christmas tunes through the speakers. What she wouldn't give to be baking cookies and watching holiday specials with her baby girl right now. And as much as she knew that heading to NASA was the right choice, the safe choice, she couldn't shake the memory of the pain in Chris's eyes as he'd told her to leave.

She knew it made no sense, that her heart had no business wishing he'd asked her to stay with him even when it wasn't the wise choice. Still, her intuition told her that staying with Chris was the right thing to do—she felt safe around him and trusted him to help her find Hayley.

Her poor daughter. Was she scared? In danger? Natasha drummed her fingers on her leg and tried to run each possibility as a simulation in her mind. Maybe Hayley had headed home in the confusion. She might have believed that was the safest course of action in the midst of the chaos. Maybe she'd gone to a bathroom in another part of the school. Maybe she'd sneaked off with a classmate to visit the corner store and buy chips or magazines. Twelve years old was old enough to start the bouts of defiant teenage behavior, right?

Natasha pressed her fingertips of her other hand into the corners of her eyes, trying to stave off the throbbing that had begun the moment they'd pulled out of the school parking lot. Why didn't anyone see Hayley leave?

Why wouldn't the school have known about a stranger on the premises? She wished Chris was there with her—he'd surely have a few ideas of his own, and they could have bounced theories off each other. Maybe he'd even talk her down and tell her that her growing suspicion was wrong. Or maybe he'd independently affirm her worries, and they'd be able to work it out together.

Because one thing was growing clearer by the minute: if Hayley hadn't left the school on her own, it meant she'd left with someone she knew.

Keep my Hayley-girl safe, Lord, Natasha prayed. *Give Chris the strength he needs to find her and bring her home to me.*

"So, you really don't remember anything?" Ward said from the driver's seat. Natasha's eyes flew open—she hadn't even realized that she'd closed them while praying. "What's the last thing you recall?"

She didn't want to go over this again, but these were her friends, and they deserved to know. "I was on my way to an appointment with the physician the other morning, and that's literally it. Everything gets hazy after that. One moment I'm driving my car, and the next I'm waking up by the side of the road with a gun by my hand, being used as target practice. It's been nonstop since then. And now Hayley's gone." Hot tears prickled against her lower lids, and this time she didn't bother to blink them away. Safe with friends and the FBI in an escort vehicle behind them, she could finally feel something. Lose the cool logic for a few minutes and simply let go.

So why did she feel more tense than ever?

"That's wild," Ward said, his voice low and harsh. "Do the doctors think you'll get your memories back soon?"

"Things are coming back in bits and pieces. It's like…when something critical happens or I see an image that evokes a strong emotion, the information breaks through the barrier in my brain. But not always."

"Do you even remember Evans and May? Or are their deaths basically meaningless until you get your memories back?"

"Ward!" From the back seat, Coulson's scolding sounded thick with grief. The woman's breathing had grown shallow, and Natasha twisted in her seat to check on her. Coulson's face was streaked with tears, black lines of mascara running down each cheek like a never-ending flood. She'd definitely allowed her emotions to take over. "Have some respect.

Please. These are our friends. You should know better."

Natasha reached back to grab Coulson's hand, and as her fingers closed around those of the other woman, she was suddenly flooded with warm flashes of memory—images of herself and Melinda Coulson prepping for takeoff, enjoying each other's company at dinner, exchanging birthday gifts. *Melinda* was more than a colleague; she was a friend.

Hope sprang anew in Natasha's heart. Even if Chris couldn't be with her, she had a trustworthy friend by her side while they hid from the world at NASA.

Melinda offered a tiny smile as Natasha squeezed her hand and turned back around in her seat. The heavily secured entryway to Kennedy drew closer—they were almost there.

"Think the FBI will leave us alone once we're in?" Ward asked.

"They're here for our protection," Natasha said, a little annoyed that Ward would dismiss their assistance so readily. "We're very privileged to be given such attention. An FBI detail is no small thing."

Ward grew silent, but Natasha didn't miss how his eyebrows knit and he looked in the rearview window with a frown. For someone who should be used to constant oversight while working at NASA—even their bathroom breaks had been scheduled down to the minute during the Orion mission—he was acting awfully cagey about a detail so minimal as an FBI escort for their own protection.

He noticed her looking at him and reached across the seats to take her hand, but she couldn't accept the gesture. She pulled her hand away as though she hadn't noticed him reaching for her, using the motion as a pretense to tuck her hair behind her ears. She thought she heard a small grunt of frustration, but she couldn't be certain. Were they truly more than friends? It still didn't sit right, but at least he wasn't forcing the issue.

They drew up to the gate and waited for security to open the doors. As they rolled through, Ward lowered his window and waved to the FBI escort to let them know they were no longer needed. As the Suburban rolled away, another lump formed in Natasha's throat. Even without Chris in that vehicle, having an FBI team nearby had felt like a solid lifeline to the one man she truly trusted right now.

It's more than trust, said a small voice inside. *And you know it.*

But did she? It wasn't possible. They'd

known each other for only a couple of days—but no, that wasn't quite true, either. She still hadn't been able to recall any memories of their past together, and she hadn't had a moment today to sit down and talk about it with Chris as they'd planned.

And Chris seemed convinced that whatever had happened, it was something they couldn't get past, but she wanted to be judge of that for herself. Once Hayley was safe in her arms and the danger had passed, they'd talk. She'd be sure of it.

With the FBI Suburban out of view, Natasha anticipated that Ward would continue into the complex, find a parking spot and they'd all head inside together—but instead he yanked on the wheel and spun the Range Rover around in a full doughnut.

"What are you doing?" Natasha braced herself with one arm against the door and the other gripping the seat. "Slow down!"

"We're not staying here," Ward growled. "I have a better idea. You think the FBI and the drone showing up around the same time are coincidence?"

"Of course not, because—"

"Someone on the inside knows where we are and where we're going to be! How else did they get to May and Evans? No one has their schedules but our own HR department. NASA has our days so tightly scheduled, which means that all that needed to happen was for one of our own people to turn against us."

From the back seat, Melinda spoke in a very tense, very quiet voice. "You guys...you don't think this has anything to do with—"

"Stop talking!" Ward snapped. Melinda pressed her lips together but caught Natasha's eyes in the rearview mirror. What Natasha saw there matched how she felt, too, reflecting confusion and concern. "We can't be sure of anything. I have a safe place for us to go. Trust me."

Natasha had no idea what they were talking about, but what he'd said about someone on the inside...that seemed like the immediate concern. "Should we call it in? Tell someone where we're going? We can't just take off—the FBI sent an escort for a reason."

Ward shook his head. "Don't you see? That's the whole point. We can't trust them. We can't even trust that agent you're working with. Think about it, Stark. When did your troubles start?"

Natasha's mouth grew dry and her forehead felt hot. Anxiety-induced perspiration broke out across the back of her neck as she thought about the past day and a half. And Ward's accusations.

And considered how someplace, deep inside, she'd been wondering the same thing all along.

TEN

Chris had to arrest Natasha.

"Should I tell the escort to turn around?" A fellow agent stood by his side, his own phone at the ready. "They can head back in there and make the arrest."

He needed to make the right call, but what *was* the right call? Natasha had been through enough, and her daughter was still missing. Even with a match on ballistics and residue, it didn't prove that Natasha had killed her fellow astronaut. The timeline didn't make sense...but the truth remained that Natasha was still missing a significant portion of her memories, and the coroner's office had made an initial estimate on Cobie May's time of death, placing it a few hours before he'd found Natasha up to a few hours after they'd been together. The estimate for Dr. Evans's time of death had been placed after that time period, making it look even more like a suicide—as if he'd either seen May's body or found out about her death some other way, then gone home and performed his final, fatal act out of despair.

It wasn't looking good for Natasha, but Chris knew there had to be a reasonable explanation. Twelve years was a long time, though. *How much do I really know this woman? She certainly seems to have changed...and she's not even the same woman now as she was yesterday morning, right after losing her memories.*

"Agent Barton. What are your orders?"

Physical guilt tore through Chris. He couldn't send someone else to arrest Natasha, not with her health issues and her daughter missing. The mental taxation of an arrest on top of everything else could do irreparable damage. Even if she *was* guilty of May's death, that was no excuse to do further harm to her health if at all avoidable. That wasn't how the justice system worked.

"Leave it," he told the other agent. "I'll make the arrest personally, as soon as we have a lead on Hayley Stark. The astronauts will be secure at NASA and under watchful eyes there. They're not going anywhere."

"But, Agent Barton—"

"I'll take the heat on this, Parker. Anyone questions my actions, send them right to me and I'll pull up ten reasons why we're delaying on making an arrest. It'll happen, but we have a missing child to find, and her mother is at a secure government facility. She's not a danger to herself or others, and she's not going to run while her child's whereabouts are unaccounted for. Understand?"

Parker nodded and walked away, appearing perturbed. Chris didn't particularly care how the other agents felt about it—this was his case, and he'd handle Natasha how he chose. And as soon as Hayley was safe, he'd find a way to explain the ballistics report.

His plan was easier made than accomplished, however. Two hours later, after searching the school grounds, the Starks' house and contacting the Kaifs and grilling them for a half hour regarding their relationship with Natasha and Hayley, he and the other agents were no closer to finding Hayley. They'd received no leads on her whereabouts. The lack of information or contact from an abductor made Chris even more nervous. Why take a child to make a point if you weren't going to contact the parent or person whom it affected, to be sure that point could actually be made?

The lack of a ransom demand or anything of the like forced Chris to consider several alternatives—that Hayley had left school on her own and was still holed up elsewhere, waiting for the furor to die down, or that something entirely unrelated to the attacks on Natasha had happened. A crime of opportunity, perhaps. Someone taking a vulnerable-looking girl in a moment of confusion. He swallowed against the dryness in his throat.

My little girl. I'm going to find you. I haven't been there for these twelve years of your life, but I can be there for you now. And even if you're not mine, I'll still fight for you. Please hold on.

But after another hour of fruitless searching and no leads, Chris felt weary to the bone.

The FBI was taking their time examining all angles, and the local police was doing as much as resources allowed, but they had other tasks to perform and didn't have a large contingent of extra available officers to help out. Neighborhood canvassing had turned up nothing. The local news had broadcast an Amber Alert for Hayley Stark, and the television provider in the area was scrolling the alert along the bottom of all local cable channels, but no relevant tips had come in. And still no contact from her abductor.

It had begun raining a little while ago, the gray skies finally opening up to pour forth and drench everyone and everything, adding an extra layer of complexity to the search. He sat in his SUV as fat droplets smacked against the windshield. At least it wasn't snow—that was one part of Christmas in the Midwest that he wouldn't miss at all. He dropped his forehead against the steering wheel as he tried once more to rack his brain for ideas. What other possible angles could he explore? He needed something fast, because he couldn't avoid his officer in charge much longer—rather, he couldn't avoid Natasha's arrest for much longer.

He flipped his phone over in his hand, fingers splaying across the smooth surface of the case and screen. Who could possibly help? Who might have any clues? Why had no one called?

God, I don't know if You'd bother listening to me after how I rejected You, but if You're there...please keep Hayley safe. Natasha doesn't deserve this. She's a good woman, and I'm afraid I've made a terrible mistake by never opening her letters all those years ago. I thought I knew her, but maybe I misjudged her...the way I'd been convinced she misjudged me when she called things off.

And then it came to him, like a firework lighting up a night sky.

He unlocked his phone and started dialing, heart racing triple time, each breath suddenly rapid and shallow. An operator answered and he asked to be transferred, and after twenty-three minutes of dealing with more transfers, waiting music and one completely dropped connection, he heard it—the voice on the other end that gave him hope, but that also filled him with nauseating, long-buried anxiousness.

"Good afternoon, Senator Stark speaking. What can I do for you today?"

The words stuck in Chris's throat at the sound of Natasha's father's voice, flooding him with memories. Dismissal and rejection surged to the surface, and he shoved them aside—there were more important things at stake than either man's ego.

"Senator Stark, thank you for taking my call. This is Agent Chris Barton of the FBI."

"Barton? Why does that name sound familiar?" A pause, followed by an exclamation of utter disbelief. "Hold on. You're not...you're not *that* Chris Barton, are you?"

Chris swallowed down a rude retort and plunged forward. "Yes, sir, I am. But that's not important. What matters is that your granddaughter is missing. Her life is in danger, and I need your help to find her before it's too late."

Natasha's head spun as Ward approached the gates of a large complex. They'd been driving slowly down the coast for ages, even pulling over for a solid forty-five minutes during a downpour that caused the Range Rover's tires to hydroplane all over the road, only to reach this place that looked very similar to the entryway setup of Kennedy Space Center. Was she seeing things? Had they been driving in a loop for the past few hours? No, the security at this place had a showier quality about it—a tower with a guard at the top, two sets of gates to pass through and cameras mounted everywhere. Armed security stood sentry on either side of both sets of gates, and charged barbed wire ringed the top of the fences. Bright lights whirled as they passed through the first gates, and a loud alarm sounded to let everyone know that visitors were arriving. Did they use all these lights and sounds for employees, too?

She checked her phone for what felt like the millionth time, but she still hadn't received an update from Chris on the search for Hayley. What if he found her in the next five minutes? It would take ages for Chris to bring her daughter to wherever Ward had driven them for safety, but every time she'd brought it up on the drive, Ward had dismissed her concerns and assured her that everything would be okay once they were secure inside his supposed safe location. She wanted to trust Ward's judgment because, after all, trust was everything on a space mission and they were a team. Still, she felt queasy as she waited for the notification light on her phone to blink.

A massive red-and-black sign towered over everything as they moved toward the second row of gates. The sign was lit by spotlights from above and below. *Iron Aerospace.* Not a "welcome to" or "you are now entering," or any kind of description of what they did here, just the name of the facility.

She stared at the sign as they passed. As she turned the name over in her mind, a seed of familiarity pushed through her mental block. It tugged on a thread of memory that refused to unravel.

"What is this place?" She craned her neck to try taking in the long, low building as they passed through the gates and made their approach to the main complex. Shiny chrome siding with black trim made a statement of wealth, similar enough to NASA to have been inspired by the government building's practical concept, but with a dramatic flair to let the visitor know that they were walking into something new, different and progressive. "Let me guess—a private company? Is that why you think it'll be safe?"

"It's why I *know* it'll be safe," Ward muttered, but Natasha hardly heard him over the concerned mumblings from the back seat.

"Melinda? What's wrong?" Natasha twisted around again to see Melinda's head whipping back and forth at the sights of the complex, her peach blush unable to hide how her cheeks had paled.

When Melinda finally responded, her expression darkened and she spoke in a near growl. "You can't tell me this has nothing to do with the Orion mission, Ward. We all knew very well who tried to make that deal. What are you doing bringing us here?"

Natasha blinked at the both of them. Her head pounded, memories still trying to surge forward as her brain struggled to make sense of the conversation. She couldn't quite grasp it. "What are you talking about? Please, one of you, fill in the blanks for me."

"You seriously don't remember?" Melinda's voice rose in pitch. She leaned forward in her seat, eyes wide and wild. "Iron Aerospace, they tried to—"

"That's enough!" Ward shouted. In the same instant, he flung his arm around the seat and Natasha heard a crackle. The air in the vehicle felt sharp and charged, and Melinda suddenly shuddered and fell backward, limbs flopping at strange angles.

A Taser! "Ward, no!"

"Too late," he said, replacing the device inside his front jacket pocket. "She was freaking out and would have spoiled this for all of us."

"Spoiled what?" Natasha concentrated on taking full, deep breaths. *In and out, in and out. Like you're on a space walk with limited time and limited oxygen. Stay in control.* "None of this is making any sense. Why didn't you let her answer my question?"

Ward grunted and hunched his shoulders as he pulled up to a side door. "I'll explain everything inside. Didn't want her getting hysterical and causing trouble. You're in danger, remember? What if she got the wrong people's attention?"

It sounded like he was grasping at straws. As soon as the vehicle came to a complete stop, she unhooked her seat belt and climbed over the seats to reach Melinda, then pressed her fingers against the other woman's neck. Her pulse was strong—a reflection of the excellent physical shape astronauts needed to be in—but electroshock of any kind was not to be taken lightly. The passenger door opened and Ward reached in to grab Coulson, but Natasha hovered protectively over the woman.

"I'll carry her," she said.

Ward raised an eyebrow. "Really? How many injuries are you already dealing with, Stark?"

It pained her to admit that Ward was correct. With a sigh, Natasha exited and came around the vehicle from the driver's side back to the passenger's side—but as she rounded the front, her eye landed on an unusual dent on its front end.

It looked like exactly the kind of dent that might be made by a bumper hitting the back of another vehicle. Her pounding heart picked up speed. Surely she was imagining things, seeing trouble where it didn't exist just because it was the same kind of SUV.

She almost kept walking. Tried to put it

out of her mind and focus on Melinda, on her daughter, on everything else that seemed more important than a dent in a vehicle. Ward looked up at her, suspicion painted across his features. She offered up a reassuring smile and kept walking.

She couldn't help it. She let her palm brush against the dent and curled her fingernails into the paint, and nearly gasped in surprise as her nails sank in and scraped lines across the burgundy finish.

The moment that Ward looked away to gather Melinda in his arms, Natasha glanced down at the lines she'd left in the paint job and wanted to scream. Underneath the shoddy, rushed and uncured red paint of the Range Rover was a navy-colored vehicle.

Ward's hand closed around her upper arm, and she snapped her gaze to him, panic rising. "Come inside, where it's safe," Ward snarled, his smile a little too forced. "We need to talk."

ELEVEN

"What do you mean my granddaughter is missing? After everything you've told me, can't the FBI do its job correctly? Titusville is not a large town. You should be blocking all the highways and sending search teams through every suburb—"

Chris gritted his teeth, trying to afford the senator as much respect as possible. He needed to be on the man's good side if they were going to make any headway with what he wanted to ask. "With all due respect, sir, we've mobilized every unit possible and we have reinforcement teams on the way in from elsewhere in the state, but the fact of the matter is that we also have two deceased astronauts from your daughter's crew, and there have been a slew of assaults on your daughter over the past forty-eight hours. Our resources are stretched to the limit, even with the assistance of the local police."

The man grunted, and Chris imagined that if he could see him, the senator would be scowling and shaking his head. "Dead astronauts, attacks, it's ridiculous. Absolute nonsense. This is why NASA and its projects are a waste of government resources. You think that there'd be all of this ludicrous business happening if it was a private company?"

"I can't speak to that, sir. And, frankly, I'm not sure how it's relevant."

"Don't get me wrong, Agent Barton. I'm glad the FBI is searching for my granddaughter. But the FBI working on astronaut deaths, bringing in more agents from out of state...it's a waste of government finances. What does NASA even bring to the table for this country? What have they done for us since the moon landing? The Space Race is over. The shuttle program was canceled years ago, for good reason—Columbia and Challenger ringing a bell, Agent? Those moneygrubbing, stuffy scientists sit around all day dreaming up flights of fancy, indulging their own nonsensical desires. No one can convince me that it's a good idea to spend this country's billions on trying to reach Mars. Let the private billionaires handle that, like that other place along the coast there… Iron Aerospace. You've heard of it?"

"Can't say that I have, sir." Chris rubbed his eyes, anxious to keep the conversation moving. If the senator couldn't be of assistance, he needed to keep pushing and find another way to get help. "And while I'm all for competition in the economy, the biggest concern right now is locating your granddaughter. That's why I've called you."

"What? What could you possibly think that I could do for you?"

Chris took a deep breath and plunged forward. "I know you have a lot of pull and connections across the state. I'm begging you to mobilize whatever resources you can, to use those connections, to help find Hayley. I can only do so much as FBI, but if you know of any tech companies, or private investigators, or other government branches that might be willing to give us a hand, please. Every minute counts. You need to understand that with two deceased astronauts, we can't rule out the possibility that Hayley was taken by someone related to these deaths—"

"The news report I'm reading says that one was suicide, Agent."

"Please, listen to me. We haven't received

any demands regarding your granddaughter, and that's not a good sign. The longer it takes to find her, the less likely it is we'll find her alive."

The senator grew silent as Chris's final words echoed through the line. A chill slipped down the back of Chris's neck at speaking the truth aloud, but there was no getting around it. Every moment that ticked by reduced the chances of finding Hayley unharmed.

Finally, the senator spoke. "I'll do what I can. For my granddaughter."

A click on the other end of the line was followed by the dial tone. Senator Stark had hung up on Chris, but not before agreeing to help. Whatever form *that* would take. It wasn't quite what Chris had hoped for, but it would have to do.

He texted a message to Natasha. He planned to call her with an update once he spoke to his officer in charge about the senator's assistance, to let him know to expect some additional involvement on the government end of things. Moments later, his phone pinged with a notification: *Unable to deliver message.* That was odd.

He typed another message, but it didn't go through, either. Bad reception? It was plausible there'd be cell reception dead zones in a fortified facility like Kennedy. He tried phoning instead, intending to let it ring as long as it took for Natasha to leave the dead zone and move to another part of the facility, but the call also refused to connect.

He stared at his phone screen, a sinking sensation in the pit of his stomach. Something wasn't right. Natasha wouldn't turn off her phone or go anywhere long term where her reception stopped working, because she was probably pacing the floors of NASA's headquarters with her phone gripped tightly in her hands, desperate for his call with more information about the search for Hayley. And with two astronauts down today already…

As soon as the thought formed, Chris jumped into his Suburban and peeled out of the parking lot, tires squealing. He hammered on the gas and sped across town toward the space center, double-tasking to phone the agent who'd headed up the FBI escort to the facility.

"Paltrow!" Chris shouted into his Bluetooth system once the call connected. "Did the assets and our team reach Kennedy?"

"Affirmative" came Agent Paltrow's voice through the speakers. "They entered the security gates and waved us on. We left once they'd pulled through into the facility."

"Great. Thank you." Chris disconnected the call as his panic abated a degree. If they'd made it onto the property, maybe he really had caught Natasha at a bad time. To reassure himself, he tried calling again. That call also refused to connect, as did every other call as he rushed across town. Less than a mile out from Kennedy, he pulled his Suburban to the side of the road and phoned the facility's front desk directly.

"Good afternoon, Kennedy Space Center. Wanda speaking. How may I direct your call?"

"Wanda, this is Special Agent Barton of the FBI. I'm looking to find out if three of your people—Stark, Ward and Coulson—arrived at the facility about an hour and a half ago. I'm not sure which area of the property they're on, but they should be there. Can you confirm?"

"One moment, please." Soft Christmas carols played through the speaker as Wanda placed him on hold. He tapped his fingers against the steering wheel, impatient and annoyed by the cheerful chimes of "O Holy Night." Some holy night of the Christmas season this was turning out to be. *Where are You now, God? Where are You when Natasha and Hayley need You the most?*

Every second counted. Hayley's life was on the line, and now Natasha... "Hello, Agent Barton?"

"Talk to me, Wanda."

"I've been told by security that these individuals did not arrive—well, they did, but they didn't stay."

They *what*? "Explain."

"Security noted the vehicle as it approached the gate. On the monitors, the security team on duty recognized Ward and Stark in the front seat, but apparently they remained in the lot for less than a minute before turning around and leaving the premises. The vehicle headed south."

Chris thanked Wanda and disconnected, then slammed his hands on the wheel. How could they have taken off like that? What would have possessed them to turn around and leave the safety of NASA's property, and to do so out of sight of their FBI escort? Natasha would never have agreed to leave, not after everything they'd gone through. But with Ward at the wheel... Natasha had already mentioned feeling strange about his behavior, though she'd chalked it up to her missing memories and not being able to remember what he was like.

What had he learned as an agent? *Always trust your gut.* And he hadn't given enough weight to Natasha's gut feelings because of her memory loss. That made this his fault, no question. If anything happened to her or Hayley, he'd live with that guilt for the rest of his life.

His phone buzzed on the passenger seat next to him, and he flinched in surprise. He grabbed it and opened a text message from a number he didn't recognize. It said only one word: *iron*.

Iron? What on earth could that mean? He tried sending a return text, but it refused to go through. A quick phone number search in the online database accessible to FBI agents brought up no results. He was still sitting at zero on this case—no, less than zero, because now he'd lost track of the woman he'd promised to protect. He had no clues, no idea where to go or what to do next.

Please, God. Even if You and I aren't speaking, I know You're looking out for Natasha.

He pressed his fingers into the corners of his eyes, trying to relieve the growing tension in his neck and shoulders that had become even more noticeable while he'd been on the phone with Natasha's father. Senator Stark had acted as Chris remembered him, curt and rude, thinking only in terms of himself and how he was inconvenienced, rather than considering the implications for others…

Chris sat straight up in his seat. Iron *Aerospace.* The senator had mentioned a private company, Iron Aerospace. Was there another company working on the same technology? It was a long shot, and it assumed much based on one vague text message, but it was all he had to go on.

And then his eyes landed on the personnel folder from NASA, jammed into the space between the passenger seat and the center console. Natasha had left it there when they'd run inside the school, and he'd been so focused on searching for Hayley and tracking down Natasha's whereabouts that he hadn't noticed that she'd left it behind. He grabbed it as an idea sprang to mind. He paged through the sheets, adrenaline pounding as he scanned Ward's and Coulson's profiles until he found what he was looking for.

Come on, come on. And then he saw it—Coulson's private cell phone number. It matched the number from the text message.

Either Coulson or Natasha had sent that message, and it implied that they were still together. How else would Coulson have had his number? It had to be a clue, a cry for help, and though it wasn't much, it was more than he'd had moments ago.

Hope sprang anew as he pressed his Bluetooth set, ready to call for backup—and then remembered that it had been his choice not to arrest Natasha immediately. He'd delayed on executing the order, intending to take the heat if there was a problem, and now she was missing. He'd followed his gut and disobeyed a direct order, and the only way his officer in charge would see his side of this was if he fixed it himself.

Whatever it took, he'd find Natasha—he hadn't found her after all these years only to lose her again.

Natasha flinched as Ward snatched Melinda's phone from her hands. Ward had taken her own phone away when she'd grabbed for it outside. After he'd left her and a semiconscious Melinda in this room, she'd only had enough time to dig through Melinda's pockets for the phone, drag the chair over to the tiny skylight window and shove it open, then stick her arm out to send a one-word message. If it had even sent at all, that was. The skies were still cloudy, and rain continued to fall, and Ward had come back just as the phone's reception icon showed one bar. She hit the side button to lock the phone before it slipped from her fingers, preventing Ward from checking what she'd done. The time on the phone had told her they'd been in this room for well over an hour. Did anyone else know where they were? So much time had passed since Hayley's disappearance, and not knowing whether her daughter had been found was tearing her to pieces from the inside.

Ward grabbed her by the arm and wrenched her down off the chair she stood perched on.

Please, God, she prayed. *Let my message go through.*

"Who did you contact? What did you tell them?" Ward tried without success to unlock the phone, and Melinda wasn't talking. His eyes flicked across the screen before he raised his arm and slammed the phone against the floor. It landed with a crack, pieces of screen flying across the tile.

"Why did you do that?" Natasha stared at the man who'd claimed to be in a relationship with her, then gestured to the cement walls that surrounded them and to Melinda, slumped in the metal chair where he'd dumped her. Her arms rested on a chrome-plated table in front of her and she blinked away the grogginess as she stirred—the first sign of movement from her friend since they'd arrived. "Why are you doing any of this?"

"I'm protecting you," he said, kicking the broken pieces of the phone out of the way. "You'll understand soon. Go ahead—eat something. I'm not a monster."

Natasha looked at what Ward had left the room to bring them. A tray on the table contained a plate of crackers, cheese and grapes, and two bottles of water.

"I'm not hungry," she said. It wasn't entirely true, but her stomach rumbled with anxiety. Had Chris received her message? Would he even be able to make sense of it?

"You'll need your strength," Ward said. "I'm not going to hurt you. I know you don't remember, but we're in this together. We're on the same team. Iron Aerospace isn't the enemy, and they never have been."

What he'd done to Melinda certainly said otherwise. In the chair at the table, the woman groaned. Natasha knelt by her friend. Melinda's head still lolled as she struggled to shake off the effects of the Taser.

"You may have done serious damage," Natasha scolded. "You set the voltage too high. She needs a doctor. This could skew the mission recovery statistics, too—NASA spent millions on each of us, and now you've caused a potential career-ending injury."

Ward grimaced. "All she needs is some water and food. She'll be fine. She'll sleep it off."

"That's not how electroshock works," Natasha snapped. Still, she took one of the bottles of water and checked the lid. It didn't appear to have been tampered with, which was confirmed as she twisted the cap and heard the plastic tabs crack. She lifted the water to her friend's lips. To her relief, Melinda eagerly accepted the water as Ward stood in the corner, scowling. "I'd appreciate if you started explaining things," she said over her shoulder. "My daughter is still missing, and you've removed my only way of receiving information about the search. If we're truly on the same team, give me a way to get those updates."

Ward crossed the room and placed his hands on the table. "I'll find out for you."

"No. I want a way to contact the outside."

"You'll bring them here. The FBI can't be trusted. NASA can't be trusted."

"Listen to yourself! You're talking about an entire government agency, plus the people who've given you a career. We're not strangers, Ward, and even if I can't recall everything, I know *you* can. Find out what's going on in the search for my daughter."

He glared at her, then backed toward the door. "Don't try any more funny business."

"How can I? You destroyed Melinda's phone and took mine." She stood, advancing on him. "I've gone through enough the past few days to know that I'm fed up with suspense, fed up with looking over my shoulder constantly. Tell me what's happening and give me a way to find out whether Hayley has been located."

Ward's eyes widened as she approached—but as his mouth fell open, she realized that he wasn't looking at her. He was looking over her shoulder at Melinda. Natasha whirled around to see Melinda awake with her hand clutching her throat. Her eyes bulged, and she leaned over the metal table, cracker crumbs spilling from her lips.

"Melinda!" Natasha bounded across the small space to reach her friend. She tilted the woman's chin skyward and stuck her fingers in her mouth to check for a blocked airway but felt nothing. "What happened? Did you see what happened?"

There came only silence from Ward. Melinda tried to cough, tried to breathe, but the only thing that came out was a wheezing gasp as her complexion changed colors and grew deathly pale. As she looked around for something to help her, Natasha's eyes landed on the tray of crackers and cheese.

Melinda has a sesame allergy. The memory came to her in a flash, and she swept the tray off the table in frustration. It clattered against the wall and fell to the floor with a clang. Then she knelt and began digging through the woman's pockets a second time, searching for an EpiPen, though she didn't remember finding one when she'd done the same thing earlier while looking for a phone.

"Get help," she shouted at Ward. "She's going into anaphylactic shock, and I can't find her adrenaline. Call 911—see if the nearest first-aid kit contains Benadryl, anything! Don't just stand there!"

As she pulled Melinda from the chair to lay her on the floor in a more comfortable position, to better open her airway, Ward merely crossed the room to stand next to Natasha.

"What happened?" He spoke as though this was a mere curiosity, not a life-and-death situation.

"What do you mean, what happened?" Natasha looked up at him in fury. "You Tased her, she was groggy waking up, probably hungry and thirsty after the rush of everything that happened today, and likely grabbed a cracker without thinking about it. Why would you bring those in here? You know she's allergic! Just like I know that you're allergic to dogs, and May can't eat bananas without breaking out in hives..."

She gasped. Her voice trailed off as memories flooded back in waves, washing over her with knowledge and images and scents that brought back a lifetime of experiences—but she had no time to dwell on any of it or to sort through the situation.

"Are you going?" If he wasn't going to help, she'd do it herself. She ran to the door and tried the handle, but it refused to budge. She pounded on the door, calling for help, and then ran to the chair underneath the window and climbed up, screaming for help. Behind her, Ward only stood silent, shaking his head. "Ward! Melinda is dying! *What is wrong with you?*"

She jumped down from the chair, stomach queasy and hope fading. Melinda's breaths had become shallow hiccups, and Natasha grew cold all over in utter disbelief at the reality of the situation. Her friend was dying, and there was nothing she could do to save her…because the other person in the room with the power to help refused to move a single muscle.

And if he's done this to Melinda, what is he going to do to me? With a scream of anger meant to surprise and unbalance him, Natasha lunged at Ward. He had to be carrying a phone, and she'd find it. Maybe there were paramedics nearby who could help, or other people in the building with a heart, or—

But Ward was faster than she'd anticipated. He backhanded her across the jaw, sending Natasha spinning to the floor in a daze, ears ringing. Her vision grew hazy, and she sensed footsteps pounding the ground around her, heard a table scraping across the floor, followed by the click of a lock and a door opening.

"Get the one behind the table out of here," Ward growled. "The boss wants me to deal with the girl. Apparently she's complaining about boredom and demanding pizza, and you know how the boss feels about complainers.

No, don't worry about the other one on the floor. She'll be out for a while after that hit."

Hope squeezed Natasha's heart. *The girl! Could it be?*

She closed her eyes. Stilled her breathing until she took only small, shallow gasps. She felt Ward's presence hovering over her. A hand gripped her shoulder and shook her, as if trying to wake her up—trying to make sure she'd really been subdued. She willed herself not to react, praying for the strength to remain calm. Had Chris received her message and understood it? Was he on his way here even now?

Chris. Wait a minute...

She'd lost so many people these past few days, their faces had kept flashing through her mind as Melinda's allergic reaction turned fatal—and for some reason, Chris's face had appeared, too. Image after image. Memories of loss. Memories of...love?

Yes, love. They'd been engaged, and she remembered the day she rejected him, choosing her father's lies over the truth of Chris's love. She'd allowed her father's prejudiced beliefs to infect her heart and push Chris away, believing the whispered voices that he wasn't good enough for her. That she deserved better. That his family would only drag hers down.

She remembered being so selfish, so wrapped up in her learned intolerance for anyone her family considered socially lower than her, that she accepted her father's demands not to tell Chris about the pregnancy—so that Chris or his "moneygrubbing, no-good family" wouldn't come after them for the baby or drag their names through the mud.

And then her father had hidden her away during the pregnancy, forced her to complete her senior year of school online so that her shame couldn't harm his political career. She'd only been allowed to go to church, where she'd at least found love and acceptance.

She'd received the very same thing from the people at church that she'd refused to give to Chris, despite his declarations of love for her. But if he truly did love her, why hadn't he responded to any of her letters?

She remembered that now, too. All the emails she'd sent to him that went unanswered. The ignored phone calls and messages she'd left. The handwritten letters she'd sent in desperation, which all came back to her. And finally his email address stopped working and she couldn't find him on social media and she'd had no way left to contact him and tell him about his daughter.

That was why she didn't want to talk to her father. He'd pushed her to remove Chris from her life, to believe that Chris was a terrible person who only wanted a slice of their family's wealth, and she'd been too wrapped up in herself—too blinded by her father's beliefs—to challenge it. She'd willingly abandoned their love. Chris had every right to be angry and upset with her, to refuse to respond to her messages. And yet he'd helped her anyway these past few days without a single complaint. Could he ever forgive her for what she'd done?

Her heart beat so loudly in her ears it was a wonder Ward couldn't hear it, too, but after a few moments, he released her and grunted, satisfied with her nonresponse. His footsteps grew distant as he left her in the cold, sparse room. Ward had to have been talking about Hayley. Pizza and boredom? Sounded like a preteen girl to her.

The moment she no longer heard the echo of footfalls in the hall outside, she took a deep breath, rose to her feet and gathered her strength.

It was time to find Hayley, get out of here and get back to Chris before they became disposable, too.

TWELVE

Chris drummed his fingers impatiently on the steering wheel as he waited for the security gate at Iron Aerospace to open and allow him inside. It was a bad habit, showing his frustration, but in a situation like this he figured he could get away with a few bad habits. The ability to remain calm and logically work through problems was only one of the many things he admired about Natasha. She probably wouldn't have acted impulsively like he just had, racing at top speed down the coast to reach this facility as fast as it was safely possible to do so. He believed he was doing the right thing, though, driven by an urgency in his gut as he felt convinced that the one-word text message had come from Natasha herself. It had to mean Iron Aerospace. If she were here, Natasha would likely have wanted to talk out all the options, to calmly and rationally examine all angles, but this was a time for decisive action. Lives were at stake. His daughter's life. *And the life of the woman I still love. No use denying that truth any longer.*

He shoved the thought aside and focused on the scene in front of him. Reddish-orange alarm lights blinked and swiveled on either side of the massive chain-link gate. He noted the barbed wire across the top and the electrical wires running along its length. A siren announced that a visitor had arrived and the gate slid open, revealing a fifty-yard pavement border between the gate he'd just come through and…was that a *second* gate?

Fancy place, he thought. It looked even more secure than the upgrades at Kennedy, which he supposed shouldn't be a surprise, considering who ran the place. As he waited for security to wave him through the next gate, he scrolled through an online information page about the facility and discovered that Iron Aerospace had been founded by Jennifer Irons, the tech genius and billionaire daughter of a former NASA astronaut. Her father had passed away after completing numerous rounds of mission training but never being given the clearance to sit on a crew, and therefore had never had a chance to live his dream of going into space. According to Irons, she'd founded Iron Aerospace in response to what she felt was wasteful expenditure at NASA and a personal desire to see space travel in the hands of the general public—so that those with a passion for space travel could live their dream without all the red tape. She wanted to commercialize space travel and see private scientists develop new technologies to benefit society as a whole, without having critical advances in the hands of the "untrustworthy" government.

Chris saw her point and agreed with her to an extent. There was nothing wrong with a little competition to spur advances in technology—after all, look what had happened during the Space Race with Russia—but there was a reason such advanced tech remained in government hands for as long as it did. Many major advancements had the potential to be dangerous at a catastrophic level, and government wasn't always out to "get" people. Chris understood both sides, the good and the bad, and he'd freely admit there were issues with government regulation. But private industry had its issues, too, and ultimately, wasn't working together the better solution for everyone involved?

As the second chain-link gate parted to allow him inside, Chris's stomach twisted with anticipation. The facility looked stark, but also reeked of wealth. Who needed chrome siding? It was blinding and impractical in the Florida heat, no matter the time of year. Still, it appeared very space-age and surely would be appealing to potential investors.

He pulled up to a large set of double doors and parked, wasting no time in heading inside. The entryway had a tall, arched ceiling with decorative, glittery silver globes that he assumed was designed to represent the solar system or a constellation of some kind. He would have loved to take a more careful look if there weren't lives at stake. Perhaps some other time.

A primly dressed receptionist sat at a low, contemporary desk. The desk itself was white, with a chrome computer screen on one side and chrome desk accessories on the other. A baseball-size reindeer figurine occupied one corner, looking rather out of place. The receptionist typed on a white keyboard that slid out from underneath the desk, and as he approached, she faced him with clasped hands and a pleasant smile.

"Welcome to Iron Aerospace, Agent Barton. How may we be of assistance today?"

Chris couldn't stop the glower from forming on his face. It seemed totally bizarre that anyone could act perky on a day like this. "I need to know if you've had a visit from anyone today."

It was her turn to frown. "We have a lot of people coming through every day. We're a scientific facility."

"You'd know if these folks were here. NASA types. Astronauts, well-known members of the community. Two women and a man." A muscle in the upper corner of her lip twitched, but she simply stared back at Chris. He wasn't buying the wide-eyed innocent routine. "I don't think I need to remind you that you're speaking to a federal agent, Miss…?"

She didn't offer her name, and she wore no name tag as identifier. Chris tried not to be suspicious—surely she hadn't removed her name tag or the nameplate on her desk before he arrived—but it seemed awfully unusual for a facility that appeared to be otherwise savvy on maintaining their appearance with impeccable detail.

"Do you have an appointment?" She ignored his question and turned back to the computer screen, typing as though checking a calendar.

Chris had no time or patience left to play

games. He rounded the corner of her desk to call her bluff and she leaped out of her chair with a squeal of alarm—then flicked up the lid of a plastic box on the wall and flailed her arm against it, slamming a red button. A whooping alarm immediately sounded as two security guards rushed into the foyer. The squealing receptionist pressed her back against the wall as the burly men approached.

You have got to be kidding me. Chris reached into his pocket and flashed his badge at them.

"Slow down, boys." The security men, who'd been reaching into their back pockets for—what? Nightsticks? Guns?—paused at the sight of the badge and Chris's casual sweep of his jacket from his side, revealing the FBI standard-issue sidearm holstered there. "I'm FBI, and I'm following a lead. If you'll all co-operate and answer a few simple questions, I'll be on my way. There are lives at stake here."

"Come back with a warrant," one of the security guards said. "Until then, get out."

Chris balked at the man. "I'm not here to search the premises. I'm here to ask a few questions."

"No one is speaking without a lawyer present," said the other.

"You realize that makes it sound as though

this facility has something to hide, right?" Chris glanced at the receptionist, whose cheeks flushed at his assertion. *Good.* She was actually listening to him, unlike the hired muscle. "If you'd just answered my first question instead of using classic avoidance tactics, I wouldn't be standing here and wondering just how long it really will take to come back with a warrant. I had no reason to search the premises before this, but thanks to the three of you… well, I'll be sure to let your boss know who it was who brought the FBI to her doorstep, hmm?"

The receptionist's throat bobbed as she swallowed and shuffled back to her desk. The security guards, however, simply advanced on Chris as though his words meant nothing.

"If you don't have an appointment, I'm going to have to ask you to leave," she said, voice wavering.

Chris glowered at the receptionist and the security guards. "This isn't over."

She said nothing as she picked up a phone receiver and pressed a button, likely to let her boss know about his visit. That was fine, let her do that—Chris would leave the reception area and let everyone cool down for a few minutes. Leaving the premises entirely, however?

Not likely, not after that rather extreme welcome. He didn't need a warrant to drive around outside a bit.

He climbed back into the Suburban and pulled the vehicle away from the front doors, intending to scout the outside of the building for any clues regarding Hayley's or Natasha's whereabouts. If they were even here. He turned the corner of the building, and about halfway down the side, he saw an open delivery door. A white van had been backed up close to the entrance. Chris pulled the Suburban forward slowly, watching as two men in jumpsuits—the type of outfits worn by mechanics or military recruits during training—unloaded crates and carried them inside.

Hope sprang anew in Chris's chest. These individuals would be less likely to put up resistance when he flashed his badge, and his intuition drove him to get inside the facility immediately.

Once he was about twenty feet away, he parked the Suburban and waited, observing how long it took for the men to unload crates, take them inside and return to the van. The third time the men disappeared inside the building, Chris jogged toward the open door.

He peered around the corner, one hand on his weapon. The way was clear.

He stepped into a long hallway with multiple doors on both sides, some open and some shut. There appeared to be another hallway about thirty feet away.

Now or never, God, Chris prayed. *I know we're not in touch very often these days, but Natasha trusts You. I want to trust You, too, because there's no way I'm getting through this alone.*

With a deep breath, he plunged into the facility. His pulse sped up as he passed the first set of doors in the hall, and the next, and the next. He was only steps away from the crossing branch of the hall when he heard steps coming from the other direction. He thought about backing up and slipping into one of the open rooms he'd just passed, but low voices floated through the air—probably the men who'd been carrying the crates.

Chris made a split-second decision and quickened his steps to cross the open hallway to the other side, then tried the first door on his left. The handle turned easily, and he slipped inside, quietly closing it behind him—until the slap of a palm against the door caused him to jump and spin around, weapon drawn.

"Chris! You got my message!"

Chris's heart soared at the sight of Natasha—and then plunged as he noticed the bright purple bruise that had blossomed on her cheek. Before he could say anything, she lunged forward and wrapped her arms around him, pressing her face to his chest. He coughed in surprise. Then he returned the gesture, holding her close, her small but muscled body comfortable against his.

"Are you all right?" he whispered, keeping one eye on the door in case the men across the hall had seen or heard either of them. "Where's Coulson and Ward?"

Her eyes grew wide as she pulled back, shaking her head. "Did you find Hayley?"

He shook his and waited for her to answer his question, though his heart squeezed at the blatant agony written across her features.

"Melinda Coulson is dead," she said, her mouth settling into a fine line, as though this was the only way she could deliver the news without falling apart. "Ward killed her. It might have been an accident, it might not. I'm still not sure either way. But… Chris?"

His breath caught in his throat. Somehow he knew exactly what she was going to say.

He could hardly find the strength to speak the word. "Yes?"

"I remember you. I remember *us*."

Natasha touched her hand to his cheek, his rough stubble scraping against her palm as he blinked at her in surprise. Yes, she'd made a terrible mistake when they were young, and she didn't blame him for not wanting anything to do with her, but that didn't explain why he hadn't returned a single email. Especially after she'd had a change of heart and defied her father's wishes three months later, telling Chris about the pregnancy in an email where she begged forgiveness for keeping it from him.

"It's all right," she said, hoping to shake him out of it. "Chris, there's no time for this. We need to get our daughter back and find a way out of here before we're next on the hit list—" She turned around to check the door and see if the way was clear, but Chris's hand was on her wrist faster than she could pull away.

It was then that she realized what she'd said. She prepared herself for a stare of disbelief—but it didn't come. Instead, he looked at her with understanding. Acceptance. He didn't look surprised at all. "You knew?"

He nodded. "I suspected. The moment you revealed her age back at the hospital."

"Why didn't you say anything?" Chris raised an eyebrow at her, and she relented. "Yes, of course, I know. It wouldn't have made sense without my memories. But...we can talk about this later, when we're safe. No one seems to be looking for me right now, but as soon as Ward gets back to that room and discovers I'm gone..."

"I have a daughter. We have a daughter. You kept it a secret from me for twelve years."

Natasha couldn't help it—her anger flared at his accusation. "I didn't! I sent letters and emails! I left messages! You weren't interested."

"I wasn't interested? How can you say that? I didn't even know you were pregnant!"

Her jaw dropped as she saw the truth in his eyes—truth that arrived in the form of tears he blinked away, real emotion at confirming that for the past twelve years, he'd been the father of a child he hadn't even known existed until yesterday.

She shook her head. "How is that possible?"

"Did your father tell you I wasn't interested? Or that I wanted nothing to do with our child? Think about that, Natasha. Think about whether I ever, in the history of knowing each other, would act like that. Did I ever give you a reason to think I didn't love you? Did I ever give you a reason to think I wouldn't act on such a massive responsibility? I didn't answer your phone calls or messages because you broke my heart. You threw me away like an old T-shirt when you thought I wasn't good enough anymore. You listened to your father's lies and chose to believe them instead of believing in us. You stayed silent when he insulted my family just because we were poor, from a lower social class. I thought we were stronger than that, but you gave up on us."

Natasha tried to swallow, but her throat was dry and her tongue clung to the back of her throat. His words were so raw, his expression full of such pain, that she could hardly bear to look at him. "We don't have time to talk all this over right now, but, Chris, I was scared. I was pregnant and scared, and my father—"

The sentence stuck in her throat. Everything within her wanted to scream and cry and call him a liar—she wanted the horrifying things he was saying to be nothing but lies and deceit from a bitter ex-fiancé—but she couldn't deny the truth of his words.

Looking back in this moment, Natasha

saw how cruel and self-centered her father had been to ask her to keep the baby a secret. And how very wrong she'd been to agree, to choose fear over truth. She hadn't even had the *chance* to tell Chris first. Her parents had been the first to learn about her pregnancy after they'd rushed her to the doctor for what they'd believed to be illness. It had been her father who'd planted the seed of doubt and told her to preserve some dignity by returning the ring and letting Chris go without argument. *Uphold our family pride*, her father had said. *You've brought enough shame on us with this baby. Don't let that boy take anything else—you know he'll want the child, and look what's happened with his own family! Do you really want your baby growing up in a home like that?*

Oh, how petty and cruel her father had been. It ran in the family, this Stark trait for deception, and she'd never wanted to be a part of it—and yet, willingly, she had been. For twelve years. She'd become the very thing she'd tried to avoid.

Chris still regarded her with pained, tearful eyes.

"I'm so sorry," Natasha whispered. She turned away from him and twisted the door handle, eager to get moving, to find Hayley and evade the reach of these dangerous people—but as she opened the door a crack, she heard the thump of footsteps in the hallway. Several people were headed their way. They needed to stay hidden. The footsteps didn't sound hurried, so hopefully they were Iron Aerospace scientists and not security guards or Ward, but she and Chris needed to proceed with care if they were going to reach Hayley and escape with their lives. She closed the door and turned the lock, keeping her voice as low as possible. "You have every right to hate me for what I've done to you. Please, we'll talk this all out as soon as we find Hayley."

"Agreed," Chris said. He flicked his gaze toward the door, likely hearing the same thing she did. In a moment, the people in the hallway would pass and they'd need to move. She tensed, ready to run, when he brushed his fingers underneath her chin, tilting her face upward. "We have a lot to talk about. But I don't hate you. I never did, and I never will. Quite the opposite, in fact."

Natasha's breath hitched at the sensation of his fingers against her skin. This time, when he looked into her eyes, all of her doubts grew muted and inconsequential.

And that was why, when he lowered his mouth to hers and paused as if asking permission, she let him in.

THIRTEEN

Memories flooded Natasha's senses as Chris pulled her closer, and she wished she could freeze that moment in time so they could stay there for more than a brief pause—but guilt crept through her belly and she pulled away, her cheeks warming. How dare she enjoy this private moment while her daughter was missing? And at any moment, Ward might discover that she'd escaped the room he'd held her in and raise the alarm.

"I'm sorry," she repeated, looking anywhere but at him. The sound of shuffling footsteps had passed. "Not now. Maybe not ever. But definitely not now."

"I understand," he replied, though his voice sounded thick with emotion, too. She sneaked a glance at him from beneath her lashes, only to find that he also was looking anywhere but at her. Did he feel as much shame and heartbreak as she did? Erasing twelve years of lies, resentment and betrayal wouldn't happen in a matter of minutes—if she even wanted that. If *he* even wanted that.

She turned back to the door, unlocked it and peered out. The hallway sounded quiet, and the door at the far end was closed. "The coast is clear. Let's head out."

"Hang on." Chris's hand gripped the door above her, and for one tense moment, Natasha thought he wanted to offer commentary about their kiss. Instead, he pushed the door closed. "The Suburban is on the other side of the exit at the end of the hall, about twenty yards off. Are you well enough to make a run for it?"

"We can't leave. I think Hayley is here somewhere."

"At this facility?"

"Yes. When Ward thought I was unconscious, he said something about 'the girl.' I don't know why he hasn't killed me, Chris. With all the others gone, I don't know why I'm still here—especially after all the drone attacks and that car trying to run us off the… Oh!"

She remembered Ward's Range Rover, the way her fingernails dug into the paint. She lifted her hand to examine her nails, seeing red flecks still stuck underneath.

"The vehicle that tried to run us off the road. It was Ward."

"You're joking." Chris pressed the heel of his hand against his forehead. "It doesn't make any sense."

"I know, but it had the same kind of dent that you'd expect from an SUV that smashed into someone else's back bumper, and some of the paint came off when I scratched it, as if someone did a really bad, hurried spray-paint job that didn't have enough time to cure. The vehicle was navy underneath, same as the one that chased us. I don't know what he's up to, but Ward's in deep."

"That's not good. You don't remember anything about your mission? Your relationship?"

Natasha sighed. That was the final missing piece of the puzzle, and yet it somehow seemed the most critical. "Not yet. Almost, though. It's hazy and just out of reach, as if one word or image will pull back the veil and let me recall everything. You…you were the biggest missing piece I've retrieved so far. Losing Melinda made me think about all the other people I'd lost, and…that included you."

With sad eyes, Chris leaned forward to plant

a kiss on her forehead. Then he reached around her to open the door again. "We should search for a security room. A facility like this has to have cameras everywhere, and if no one has spotted us already, they undoubtedly will when we start roaming the halls. On the other hand, if Hayley is here, we'll have a better chance at finding her quickly if we can scan the live feeds."

Natasha agreed with him and peered out the door. The hallway was still clear. She slipped out, and Chris followed behind. She scanned the ceiling and the corners for security cameras while he led them through the facility, stopping at each corner to check if anyone was coming.

"Where is everybody?" he asked after they'd cleared the third hallway without incident. "I thought there'd be a lot more people here."

Natasha pointed inside a room as they sneaked by, ducking underneath the window on the door. "They're working. This is a private facility, remember? This is the middle of the workday, and much of the research done in this wing of the building is probably of the deep concentration variety. Sensitive materials, total focus, that kind of thing. I'm sure once we get closer to the fabrication wing there will be more than enough noise, but not up here."

"Where were you held? Near here?"

She ran her hands through her hair, resisting the urge to grab it by the roots and tug. When would this nightmare end? "I honestly don't know. I didn't go far before I ran into you, though there was a small window facing outside. That's how I managed to get my message out."

"Good thing you did. Hold on—someone's coming." He stretched his arm out to halt her advance, then waved at her to back up. "Quickly! It sounds like they're running. We need to find an empty room or—"

"Hello, Natasha." Natasha yelped at the sound of Ward's voice approaching from the other end of the hall. Chris spun around with an expression of grim frustration. "Funny, I was just on my way to raise an alarm about your disappearance when I received a call about two unidentified personnel passing through the research wing. You're not as careful as you think you are. Your daughter takes after you, Stark. She clomped around the halls in the school as carelessly as you're doing here. It was easier to get you into my vehicle, though. I didn't even need to Taser you to keep you quiet. Good thing we didn't need to get anything from the trunk on the drive here, or that might not have been the case."

Dread and rage crept up Natasha's spine. He'd taken Hayley? He'd Tased her…and Natasha had been in the vehicle all that time with her unconscious daughter only a few feet away in the *trunk*?

"It's a large facility," Chris murmured, his calm tone the only thing keeping her from lunging at Ward and tearing him apart. "Someone was bound to notice us or we were bound to miss a camera."

"He carries a Taser," Natasha said, and this time she spread her arms wide to stop Chris from approaching Ward. "Don't get in range."

Ward laughed, a humorless, dry sound. "I'm not going to Taser you, sweetheart."

"I'm not your sweetheart. And if you Tased my little girl, there's nothing sweet headed your way."

"You think so?" When she didn't respond, Ward frowned and squinted at her as though trying to read her mind. After a tense moment, he raised his eyebrows and shook his head. Then he pulled his Taser out of his pocket and turned it over in his hands. "Well, I'll be. That changes things."

Was it her imagination…or did Ward sound a little bit sad? "Where's my daughter?" When he didn't respond, she repeated the question, louder and with greater force. "Where is my daughter, Ward? What have you done with her? You can't be all right with this. You know her! You gave her a birthday present, a book about Floridian wildlife, and offered to take her bird-watching in the Keys."

Ward flinched, and Natasha felt a small burst of hope. Chris's hand landed on her shoulder and squeezed in support, but Ward noticed the gesture and his features hardened once again. He withdrew a phone from his other pocket and held it to his ear. "Yes? I have them. Fine."

"We should run for it," Chris whispered behind her. "This man is unstable."

Natasha nodded her agreement, but something inside of her told her to wait. Ward knew where Hayley was—she felt sure of it. She sensed Chris start to pull away from her, but she remained rooted to the spot. At the same moment, Ward extended his phone toward them on an upturned palm.

"Ms. Stark? Please don't rush off." A woman's voice spoke through the phone's speaker, echoing in the metallic hallway. "For your daughter's sake, stay a moment. It's about time we had a little chat."

Chris gripped Natasha by the shoulders as she swayed backward, stumbling into his chest. The woman's voice on the other end of the line didn't sound familiar, but he could make a fairly strong assumption about who was speaking.

"Allow me to introduce myself," said the woman. "My name is Jennifer Irons. From what I've heard from Ward, you probably don't remember me."

He squeezed Natasha's shoulders again, silently begging her to remain quiet. He wished he could hold her close to make the rest of the world melt away. But she'd pulled away from their kiss—what had he been thinking, kissing her like that? They had twelve years of misconceptions and heartache to talk over first, not to mention the entire life of a child he hadn't known existed...a daughter kept secret from him on purpose, a decision initiated by the very man he'd phoned for help only a few hours ago. The knowledge that Senator Stark had been the inciting force to keep Chris from ever knowing his daughter certainly didn't give him confidence that Natasha's father would come to their rescue. Not with Chris doing the asking. They were on their own.

Still, he couldn't help but wonder—was he in the wrong for having never listened to her messages? For never having read her emails? *You agreed to never be in contact with the Starks again*, said a small voice inside. *You returned her letters and deleted those messages because you believed she'd rejected you on her own, and you couldn't afford the risk of her father making good on his promise to send you to jail. Your pride made you start to believe her father when he called your family worthless, lazy trash. You'd thought she'd bought into his toxic prejudice and cut her from your life with ruthless efficiency.*

Regret washed over Chris like a tidal wave. His pride had closed his ears to the same truth he'd just tried to convince Natasha of. *You're at fault, too, Barton. Maybe more than anyone else. You didn't even try to fight for her. One man's lies can't separate a great love, but we both let it infect our hearts and turned us against each other of our own accord. Neither of us can blame her father for that.*

"I know her," Natasha whispered, soft enough that only Chris could hear. "I know her. I remember that voice…everything… It's all there."

Chris's throat constricted. He would rejoice with her at the restoration of her memory, if it didn't sound like those memories had just put everything into a much more dire perspective.

"Now, here's the thing, Stark," said Irons. "I have a task for you, and you're not going to want to complete it. I thought you did—I thought your whole crew did—but every single one of you failed me and believed you were smart enough to outsmart me at my own game. Well, here's a news flash. I'm the smartest person in this building—possibly the country—which means that any action you think you might take, I'm one step ahead of you. How else do you think I was able to plant Ward at the school to grab your daughter? Say hello to Mommy, darling."

Natasha's next breath was a strangled cry as Hayley's voice shot through the speaker. "Mom? What's going on? Are you there?"

"Hayley!" Natasha lunged forward, out for blood, but Chris pulled her back and wrapped his arms around her torso. If she harmed Ward, who was clearly in this woman's pocket, who knew what might happen to their daughter?

Their daughter. Chris swallowed down a

wave of nausea. *His* daughter. They were all going to get out of this in one piece.

"Give me back my daughter!" Natasha screamed, choking back tears. Any semblance of calm was long gone. "Don't you touch her!"

Through the phone speaker, Irons laughed. "I'm not going to hurt her, Stark. Not so long as you cooperate for once, and this time, actually follow through. When I offered you and each of your team members five million dollars apiece to sabotage the data collected on the Orion mission's new ion propulsion system, I wasn't indulging a flight of fancy. I intend for Iron Aerospace to be the first to complete this technology and run a successful test mission, because I intend to hold the patent. The rest of the world will have to come to me, and I will stand on the shoulders of giants as the woman who enabled the first manned mission to Mars. Can you imagine it, Ms. Stark? You could be standing next to me, or on Mars as the very first human to step foot on its surface. You will be the next Neil Armstrong. The next Buzz Aldrin. Iron Aerospace will be worth billions, and you and your daughter will never have to concern yourself with cash flow or saving for the future. You could finally move out of that sad little condominium you call home.

You could send Hayley to the best schools, afford the best education for the rest of her life.

"I thought you'd already agreed to this, Ms. Stark, to be quite frank. I thought your entire crew was willing to play ball, but you changed your minds. What on earth could have possibly made you think you were smarter than me?"

Natasha's breathing grew shallow, but Chris refused to let go.

"Nothing on Earth," she finally said. "Because we weren't on Earth. In the vastness of space, we gained perspective. We realized that the easy action was the wrong action. Five million dollars isn't worth it if it means selling our integrity."

"Not all of you. Ward certainly understood the value in my proposition."

"Ward..." Natasha stared at the man, whose hard jaw and angry eyes bored into Chris as though only he was the enemy. Although Natasha hadn't said it outright now that her memories had returned, Chris had to assume that the man had been lying about having a relationship with her. His expression reflected jealousy and possessiveness, and Chris couldn't help but wonder whether that was the reason Natasha still lived. Had the man been ordered to kill his crew members and hesitated when it came to the woman he'd grown obsessed with?

"Be careful," Chris whispered in her ear. "Try to appeal to the side of him that cares for you. We might still be able to reach him."

But Natasha shook her head as she spoke. "Ward… I don't understand. I remember now—I recall it so clearly. We all agreed. We made a pact. You volunteered to infiltrate this facility as a friendly when we returned to Earth, while the rest of us stalled our meetings and gathered evidence to expose Irons's blackmail. You were supposed to be gathering internal evidence to help our case—not become a right-hand lackey. We trusted you. *I* trusted you."

Ward scoffed and turned his face to the ceiling. "Five million dollars, Natasha. You heard her. We make decent money but we don't get paid like kings, despite the dangerous work we do. Despite being so critical to national progress. Five million dollars goes a long way, and to be the first people on Mars? We'd be fighting off hordes of journalists for decades. There would be bidding wars for our life stories, for exclusives with the first humans to walk on Mars and successfully live in deep space for months at a time. We'll be the ones to skyrocket the United States to the forefront of world scientific development. There won't be another Space Race, because *we'll* already have won it."

"Is your integrity really worth that little? What's the point of being rich and famous if you've sold out your soul and betrayed your country?" Ward only shrugged, though Chris noted that the man cringed ever so slightly at the implication of being called a traitor. "You won't get away with it."

It was Ward's turn to laugh this time, though the noise lacked humor and sounded more like the nervous chattering of a man who'd started to doubt his own truth. "I already have, Natasha. Who's going to speak against me? There's only one other person besides me who knows about the blackmail, and that's you. And who do you think the NASA psychologists are going to believe? Me, a respected scientist, or you, an astronaut fallen from grace? You killed one of your crew members, causing another one to take his own life out of heartbreak. You didn't come back from your six months in space intact, and I assure you, I'll do an excellent job of convincing our medical team that I, too, have suffered. NASA's deep-space technology will be scrapped and they'll have to go back to the drawing board, believing that their product has severe, adverse psychological effects on space travelers. Something like… elevated carbon dioxide levels like in the Zarya module on the International Space Station back in 1999. There's precedent. I only need to tell a convincing story and *bam!* Any research we've done for NASA will be thrown out the window, clearing the way for Iron Aerospace."

A sickening sense of dread settled in Chris's stomach. This plan had been well thought through, with every angle covered—except for Natasha. And he needed to know why. "If you're so intent on destroying all credibility, why is Natasha still alive?"

Ward's gaze flicked to him in surprise, as though the man had forgotten there was someone else in the hall with him and his former coworker. "She's alive, because…" The man snapped his mouth shut, eyes flicking to Natasha and back.

"Because you're in love with her—is that why?" Natasha stiffened in Chris's arms. "You had orders to kill her, too, didn't you? And you couldn't go through with it."

"Ward's feelings for his coworker have made this difficult, yes," Irons said through the phone. "He disobeyed a direct order in our agreement and allowed her to live after she refused to come on board with our plan. I allowed him the opportunity to recruit her back into taking the original offer, but she refused. Under those circumstances, he was supposed to remove her from the equation, but he took matters into his own hands and decided to frame her for May's death instead. I did my best to handle the situation, but, Agent Barton?"

Chris gritted his teeth through his response. "Yes?"

"You're a much better shot than your records give you credit for."

"You promised to stop shooting at her after I told you about the amnesia," Ward spit at the phone. "You weren't supposed to send the drone to the school. You told me I could bring her in, so I did."

"My mistake," Irons chimed. A shiver ran down Chris's spine. The woman didn't sound sorry at all—in fact, it sounded more like she viewed the situation as a bit of a joke.

That, above all else, was the scariest of all. They weren't facing down a brainless criminal who reacted on impulse. They were facing an enemy of incredible intelligence, planning and skill—an enemy who dealt with tenuous situations with logic and precision. The upside here was that the FBI trained its agents to handle highly capable criminals, so he wasn't a stranger to the concept of an intelligent enemy—but he'd truthfully never had to engage with an individual of Irons's caliber.

"Clearly, however, the memory loss is no longer an issue," Irons said. Ward pressed his lips together, and Chris understood the implication. Cooperation was henceforth a requirement with whatever Irons was about to ask Natasha to do. And his life? Well, it seemed to be a nonissue, since Irons hadn't even brought his fate into the conversation yet. Did she plan to kill him or use him as a pawn? He needed to tread carefully in the next few minutes.

"Give me back my daughter," Natasha said. "And we'll leave peacefully. You'll never hear from me again. Whatever you want."

"Whatever I want? Glad to hear it. But leaving peacefully isn't an option, is it? I know you've already realized that, Agent Barton." He didn't respond. The less she thought about him, the better. "Stark, it's time for you to redeem yourself. I won't harm Hayley, so long as you do something for me in return. The data stored at Orion Mission Control remains a thorn in my side, as it is bound to undermine my own efforts. I need it destroyed, or at the very least sabotaged until it is no longer usable. How you accomplish this is up to you, but I require evidence of your success."

"Fine," Natasha agreed. Chris's heart lurched, but he understood—she'd agree to anything if it meant getting her daughter back. "Give her to me, and I'll go right now."

"Absolutely not. Once I receive confirmation of a job complete, you'll reunite with Hayley." Irons cleared her throat as Chris thought through the implications of her words. Of course she wouldn't let them go—they'd immediately contact the police. The logic didn't follow. "If you contact the police, the FBI or speak to anyone in the media regarding myself, what I've asked of you or what has happened here today, your daughter will die. Do you understand?"

"Yes," said Natasha, her voice wavering.

"And once I release your daughter, should she say anything to the media, law enforcement or anyone at all, she may find that those two beautiful children she babysits may no longer require her services."

A chill ran down Chris's spine, and this time, Natasha couldn't hold back her gasp—but of greater interest and shock to Chris was the twist of disgust on Ward's lips. The man appeared to be horrified by Irons's suggestion.

"You would kill innocent children?" Natasha pulled against Chris's grip. "They have nothing to do with this. You already put them out of their home, made the family homeless during Christmas, of all times. Why involve them at all?"

Irons's laugh was harsh and cruel. "I didn't involve them, Stark. You did. And if you and your daughter's desire to keep them alive ensures your cooperation, all the better. Don't think you'll be able to sneak around and contact the police without my knowing, either. You've seen my work. You know very well I can reach anyone, anytime, anywhere. If I so much as catch a whiff of an indication that you've spoken to anyone about this, I will act swiftly and without hesitation. And besides, Ms. Stark, it isn't as though the police are going to take you seriously if you go to them—you've become a murder suspect. Isn't that right, Agent Barton?"

Natasha did twist around this time, breaking free of his grasp. She stared at him, questions pouring from her gaze.

Irons continued. "This will make your job

somewhat more difficult, but I believe you're smart enough to find a way."

With a click, the call disconnected. The three of them stood there, silent and staring at the phone in Ward's hand. After several moments, he closed his fingers around it and tucked the phone in his pocket. Then he looked up at them, a raw sadness in the deep lines around his mouth and the creases of his forehead. He appeared to have aged ten years in five minutes.

"I know you're not going to believe me," he said, and Natasha huffed in response. "But she's gone too far."

"Too far?" Natasha raised her arms and gestured wildly to the space around them. "*This* is too far? She ordered murders of our friends, which you carried out for financial gain, and now you say she's gone too far?"

Ward shook his head. "I didn't sign up for killing children. I won't be a part of that."

"But you already *are*."

"No." His gaze snapped between Chris and Natasha. "I know you don't believe me, but she's gone too far this time, and I refuse to be a party to murdering children. She told me she wanted to take Hayley to encourage you to cooperate, but I promise you I had no idea she'd make threats on her life or the lives of other children. Hate me if you want. Don't believe me if you want. I need this money, and I need the job Irons promised, but not like this." He lowered his gaze, then covered his eyes with his hand. "Go."

"Excuse me?" Natasha glanced at Chris, but he'd heard the same thing.

Ward pulled his hand away and glared at them. "I said, go! Find Hayley and get out of here. Tell your neighbors to leave the state. It's the only way you'll all get out of this alive. You know that, right? She has no intention of letting you live once she's got what she wants out of you. Especially not you, Agent Barton. I'm surprised you're still standing." He shook his head and Chris reached for Natasha's hand, gently pulling her back toward him. "Get out of Florida—get out of the United States if you can. I know you don't believe me, Natasha, but I do love you. I tried to keep you alive as long as I could. Grab your daughter and go, before Irons realizes what you're doing. She's in the storage room next to the staff lounge, but you'll never reach it while Irons's security knows where you are. You'll have to disable the security cameras first. Go!"

Chris didn't hesitate, but Natasha did. She

remained rooted to the spot, motionless in her disbelief. He squeezed her hand and pulled, forcing her to back down the hallway with him.

If they were going to find Hayley and get out of this building alive, they were going to need speed and stealth—especially if Irons had more tricks up her sleeve.

"Where are we going?" Natasha said as they ran down hallway after hallway, turning left and right, scanning for any clue that might lead them to Hayley's whereabouts. "We should keep looking for the security room."

"Agreed," Chris replied, taking the next left. The hallways looked different here, wider and brighter, as if they'd entered a part of the facility that had been added on afterward. Not a great sign. They needed to make their way toward the center and get away from these outskirt wings. Irons probably had Hayley someplace close and central.

An alarm blared, blasting out of speakers above and around them. Chris growled in frustration—their head start was over. He paused, needing to think. Running blindly around corners wasn't working. He had a vague concept of which direction to head to get to the inside of the facility, but every hallway looked the same, and he couldn't bear the thought of bringing Natasha into even more danger. The way she looked at him right now, trusting him with her life and the life of her—*their*—daughter, urged him to prove that he was worth it. That his love for her was real, that he'd never walk away from her again—that he'd always stand up to anyone who tried to come between them, no matter whom.

Wait—love? Yes, love. Stuff his pride; forget old hurts. He loved her and he always had, no matter how hard he'd tried to convince himself otherwise through the years.

He decided to follow a gut instinct. "This way," he said, though his words were drowned by the cacophony of the alarms overhead. Natasha caught the direction he pointed and nodded, following him around the next corner.

And then they stopped dead in their tracks.

They hadn't heard their pursuers' approach over the alarms—and by trying to head into the center of the facility, they'd walked right into a trap.

Directly in front of them, thirty feet away and advancing rapidly, was a wall of armed security guards with guns aimed straight at them. And they looked angry.

FOURTEEN

Natasha's heart leaped into her throat. There were so many guns! Hayley had to be down that hallway, or at the very least they had to be on the right path.

"This way—this way!" Chris tapped her arm and turned around as the report of the first shot echoed through the hallway. Natasha felt the zip of hot lead across her knuckles, and she suppressed a scream. She wouldn't give Irons the satisfaction.

Chris pulled her around the corner opposite the one they'd come from, then drew his own weapon. Natasha's heart pounded fast enough inside her chest that it felt like bullets already peppered the inside of her rib cage—how could they possibly get out of this alive? How could they possibly find Hayley and get her away from Irons? And what kind of narcissistic sociopath threatened the lives of children, innocent kids who had nothing to do with the situation—children Irons had brought into this mess herself by virtue of her own gross incompetence in bombing the wrong condo?

The one glimmer of hope, the one thread that Natasha clung to as Chris returned fire at the armed men—one shot, two shots, and then they were off again to the next corner as the security guards advanced, coming too close for comfort—was the firm knowledge that God was with them. Even in this situation, she saw His hand at work. How else could she explain Ward's change of heart? The man had killed his close friends and coworkers in cold blood and, by all accounts, should not have let them go. He should have killed her, too, many times over, and each time she'd escaped with her life.

God is in control, she repeated to herself, taking deep breaths to fight the dizzying waves of adrenaline. *I will not be shaken.*

Chris gripped her hand and squeezed. "They're getting too close again. We need a better plan. I'm almost out of ammunition and there's no way I'm going to be able to take them all out like this. Here they come!"

They ran around the next corner, only to discover that half the guards had circled back around the other side. They were blocked on two fronts, leaving only one path that appeared to lead even farther away from the center of the building. It was clear that these men were highly trained in tactical maneuvering, so what other choice did they have?

She looked at Chris and nodded, letting him know that she trusted him. If what he'd said was true, if he truly hadn't known about the pregnancy…that changed everything.

They'd both gone through the last twelve years living a lie, a sham of a life crafted by their own pride, spurred on by her father, whose career and public image were more important than anything else. It was partially his fault that his granddaughter had grown up without a father, but she was just as much to blame. She'd chosen to let fear and prejudice win. Sure, she'd been young, but she should have known better, and she imagined Chris would say the same.

Tears sprang to her eyes, and she pushed them back. Well, no more. They were going to find Hayley and lay everything on the table. If Chris didn't want to be involved in Hayley's life, that was fine. She'd let him go, if that was what he wanted. They'd figure it out after they had Hayley. After they were safe.

After Natasha had had a chance to mourn everything she'd lost.

At the next corner, Chris huffed in frustration beside her. Bullets zipped past her face; one sliced through a strand of hair, sending it floating gently to the floor in stark contrast to the urgency of the moment.

The security team had broken off again and circled around to get ahead of them. They were cornered, and there was no way out.

"Natasha," Chris said, his voice cracking as he fired off another round at the nearest guard. And then his gun clicked.

They were out of ammunition and out of time.

Natasha backed against the wall behind them, instinctively cringing to make herself into as small a target as possible. It was over. They'd failed. One more shot and they'd be another casualty of Irons's narcissistic ambitions. She didn't even have any tears left, only a fierce prayer that God would keep Hayley safe and send someone else to take care of her daughter. As long as Hayley made it out alive and lived the life she deserved, Natasha could face death with dignity, the same way she tried to do every day while serving her country as an astronaut. She slid her hands behind her back to brace for what was to come, but her fingers brushed against cold, smooth metal. It felt like a round…knob?

She gripped it and twisted, then stumbled back an inch at the immediate give of the door. In the space between one breath and the next, she kicked the door open with her heel, grabbed the back of Chris's shirt and yanked just like Fin had the day before to pull them both backward, tumbling into the open doorway as bullets whipped through the space where their heads were less than a second before. Natasha rolled sideways to clip the door with her toe and slam it shut as Chris leaped to his feet, gripped the corner of a metal shelf standing next to the door and shoved until it toppled sideways. Boxes and equipment crashed to the floor as it fell. Natasha helped Chris to wedge the shelf under the door handle, then ran to secure two additional exits on opposite walls.

Only then did Natasha stop and turn around to see where they'd ended up. She gasped, first in surprise and then in pain.

They were in a massive hangar, but instead of housing an aircraft, this hangar housed a satellite. She stared at it in disbelief. A satellite, sitting right in front of them. It stood about as high as two shipping crates and as long as a truck trailer, rounded and paneled with silver-gray siding. The Iron Aerospace logo was stamped prominently in the center. Several of the panels were not yet shut, exposing some of the wiring and inner workings.

"I know what we can do," she said breathlessly. "I know how to get us out of here."

Chris gripped her arm and forced her attention on him. "Natasha. You're bleeding."

She followed his gaze and saw a dark red stain spreading across the right edge of her abdomen. Funny, she didn't feel a thing. "So I am—but so are you."

It was Chris's turn to look as she pointed to a similar red stain spreading across his upper thigh—but when she looked back at him, it was clear he already knew. "We need to stop the bleeding for both of us," he said. "It's not going to take long for them to get inside here. So whatever you're planning to do, you'll need to do it quickly."

Then she felt it—a warmth near her stomach that didn't feel quite right, almost as though it was on the verge of turning into pain but held off thanks to the adrenaline that coursed through her veins. "You'll cover me? I don't know how long this is going to take, but if

Irons thought cornering us in that hallway was a good idea, she has another think coming. I'm an engineer first and an astronaut second, and I know how these things work."

"These things? Satellites?" Chris pulled off his shirt and set to work tearing it into strips. He tied one around Natasha's waist and she winced at the pressure. He was right—she needed to move quickly before her brain caught up with her body. He tied another strip around his leg. "What is it exactly that you plan to do?"

She almost laughed as she scanned the underside of the satellite and found exactly what she was looking for—a control panel, accessible from the ground and therefore easy for the satellite's engineers to work on with solid footing. Satellites were massive but delicate things.

She glanced over her shoulder at the items that had fallen off the first shelf they'd toppled. Wrenches, wire cutters and other various pieces of equipment were now scattered across the floor. So long as Chris could retrieve what she needed, she could make it work. She *would* make it work, and in the process, make enough noise that they wouldn't need to contact law enforcement and risk Hayley's life—instead, law enforcement and the media would come to them and bring the eyes of the entire national public with them.

Then Irons wouldn't be able to hurt Hayley or them, but her plan was a long shot and there was no guarantee that help would arrive in time. Not like they had any other options left, though.

"You're out of ammo?" she asked Chris.

He nodded. "I can throw wrenches and screwdrivers at these guys if they break through the door, but I don't know how long I can hold them off. I've got an accurate throwing arm, but I'm only one person against many, and I don't know how far that strategy will get me with this injury. But believe me when I say that I'm not going to let them take us down quietly. We've only just found each other again, Natasha, and I don't intend for anything to separate us." His cheeks reddened as her heart began to soar, despite her own reservations. Apparently, her heart had made a decision that her mind hadn't caught up with. "That is, if you'll have me back in your life."

She opened and closed her mouth, unsure of the right thing to say.

"I know, I know," he said before she came up with a suitable response. "This isn't the time.

Go, do your thing. But aren't you going to tell me what it is you're doing?"

She nodded, allowing her eyes to roam over the smooth surface of the satellite. It truly was a thing of beauty. Millions of dollars had likely gone into its creation, thousands of hours of detailed technical work.

She looked back at Chris and smiled. "I'm going to blow it up."

"Tell me I've heard you wrong. Please tell me I've heard you wrong."

She shook her head, and a pit opened in his stomach. "We need emergency services and the media to rush to the building, as fast as possible. If it's just law enforcement, Hayley will be in more danger than she already is. This satellite is definitely Irons's next major launch from Iron Aerospace, and a massive explosion at this facility will bring everyone and their grandmother speeding down here."

"But we're in here, too." When she didn't say anything, he understood. If their lives were forfeit, so be it. As long as Hayley was safe and justice was served, that was what truly mattered. How was Natasha so peaceful about this? Was this what it meant to have faith? "What do you need me to do?"

She glanced around the hangar. "Can you try to disable the security cameras above the doors? We can't get the ones up on the ceiling, but the longer it takes for Irons to see what I'm doing, the better. If she realizes I'm tampering with the satellite, we'll have seconds. I'm banking on having minutes because she thinks we're cornered."

"Got it. Get started." Natasha turned to the satellite control panel, and he limped across the room to work on disabling the cameras. It took every ounce of willpower to drag a chair to each door and step up onto it. The wound in his leg grew more painful by the second, and putting additional stress on it by climbing up and down on a chair only exacerbated the injury. He swung a heavy wrench from the shelving unit at each camera, shattering the lens on contact.

He climbed down from the chair after smashing the last camera and stumbled, his leg giving out beneath him. With a grimace, he braced against the floor and forced himself upright.

"Do you see a small screwdriver? I'm almost there." Natasha's voice was breathless and thin, a reflection of how rapidly they were both running out of time. Even if the Iron Aerospace security didn't manage to break through, the excruciating pain from their bodies finally feeling the effects of the hits they'd taken might incapacitate them before the task was complete.

He searched the floor for a small screw-driver, then slid it over to Natasha. She bent to pick it up and he didn't miss how she gritted her teeth together, her face a contorted mask of agony. How he longed to hold her in his arms and make it all go away.

"What else can I do?" he said, his own voice also frail and harsh to his ears. But even as the words left his lips, he heard it—the slam of a heavy object against the nearest door. "I think they've figured out what you're doing."

"One more adjustment," Natasha said. "I want to give us a chance to at least try and get out of here, but it's going to be tight. I'm not sure how much time I can buy us, but it can't be too long in case—"

A clanging, rattling noise came from the top of the hangar bay door. Chains began to move, sliding across massive metal tracks at least a hundred feet above their heads.

"What's going on?" He wanted to ask for more details, but the words died on his lips as light filtered through a crack in the bottom of the now-rising hangar door.

"A few seconds more," Natasha murmured.

"Step away from the satellite, Stark."

Chris's insides convulsed. The one bright moment of hope they'd had extinguished like a candle flame snuffed out in a single breath. If his leg wasn't injured, he'd run at the woman. If he hadn't been out of ammunition, he'd have taken a shot the moment he had her in his sights.

But the truth was that both of these things meant he stood there, useless and defeated, as the hangar bay door rose to reveal the most horrifying image they'd seen all day.

Jennifer Irons stood outside the hangar with a smile on her face and a gun pressed against the temple of a trembling Hayley Stark.

FIFTEEN

Beside him, Natasha immediately dropped her hands from the satellite. He stole a glance at her. Her face had drained of color, her eyes wide like a prey animal caught in oncoming headlights. She raised her hands and moved forward slowly, as though any sudden movement might set Irons off. Chris wasn't so sure that assessment was far off, but he too took small steps to keep up. It seemed that Natasha was deliberately moving away from the satellite, toward the far outer edge of the hangar bay's entrance. Ward, on the other hand, stood back from Irons and Hayley, looking cowed. For all the evil the man had done, he'd tried to help them escape, and for that, Chris was grateful.

That didn't mean Chris excused any of Ward's actions. But it did mean that they might still be able to appeal to his humanity—especially considering the disgust that twisted Ward's lips when he caught sight of the gun pressed against Hayley's temple.

"I'm usually a very patient person," Irons said. "But I feel as though I've given you more than enough chances, Stark. How many people can say they get second chances the way you have? I was really hoping you'd come to your senses and leave that cesspool of wasted potential you call a job. Here, with me, I can make you famous. I can make you important, someone who actually matters. What are you there? Just another cog in the wheel of government interests. And let's face it—after today NASA will be even more useless. How's your father doing, Stark? Better than your uncle, I hope."

Chris winced at the implication, the insult to the Stark family. He knew about her uncle's case from the daily FBI briefings a number of months back, but she probably didn't realize he knew.

For his benefit, Natasha clenched her raised hands into fists and explained. "The vice chairman of the Joint Chiefs of Staff," she said, a tremor in her voice. "The general who was arrested for running a black-ops team and channeling funds from the Department of Defense into a private account, and who got caught after taking out a hit on a private civilian… One of your own brought him in. I'm sure you've heard of the case. That was my uncle, my father's brother. My father is trying very, very hard to keep his nose clean as a result. People in DC are keeping a close eye on him. He's walking a fine line right now."

No wonder the man had been exceptionally abrasive. "What does Natasha's father have to do with this? Or her daughter, for that matter? Come on, Irons. Let the girl go. We can talk this out peacefully. She has nothing to do with what's happening here. She's innocent."

Irons shook her head and pulled the girl back, farther away from him and Natasha as they slowly advanced. "I don't think so. No twelve-year-old is innocent, Agent Barton. And her grandfather will surely be even more infuriated with NASA once he loses both his daughter and granddaughter, thanks to the effects of deep-space travel on an astronaut's well-being. Poor Natasha Stark, psychologically unstable and guilty of murder. And of taking her daughter's life, too! I don't imagine it'll be hard to convince Senator Stark to use his influence over the senate committee in charge of

NASA funding to slash their budget even further. Maybe cripple operations entirely."

"You would honestly take the life of a child in order to further your own company's efforts?" Chris couldn't keep the disbelief from his voice. The time for remaining calm about this was long past. They were stuck in a no-win situation, because judging by the grim set of Natasha's jaw, she hadn't been able to finish the job on the satellite before Irons had entered the hangar. And yet the rest of her body language suggested they needed to get out of there.

"I'll do whatever I need to," Irons said with a sigh. "I've worked hard to make this company what it is today, and I'm not about to let someone else destroy it."

"I don't want to destroy it," Natasha snapped. "I want my daughter back. I want my life back."

"You gave all that up when you thought you could double-cross me. If you were going to back out of the deal, you shouldn't have taken it on in the first place. See how that works? Really, this is all your own fault. You did this. I'm not the one holding the gun to your daughter's head, Stark. *You* are. You're the one who's going to pull this trigger."

"Mom?" Tears streaked down Hayley's face, but the girl remained calmer than many FBI agents Chris had worked with. She held her body rigidly, but he also noticed her scanning the space around them, looking for an advantage. The thought of this girl, his daughter, looking for a tactical solution in the midst of imminent danger brought a surge of hope and pride.

That hope vanished just as quickly as Ward stepped forward. "Why do you need to kill the girl?"

"Shut up, Ward." Irons's voice dropped to a low growl. "The less you say, the better."

"But…look, I'll deal with her. I'll drop her in some country where she doesn't speak the language, someplace remote that she can't get home. Put her to work in a factory—I don't know. There's no need to kill her."

"Please don't hurt my baby," Natasha choked out. She rushed at Irons, reaching the threshold of the hangar bay before Irons reacted.

"Both of you, stop talking." Irons swung the gun away from Hayley's head toward Natasha—and then toward Ward. "On second thought, I'll shut you up myself. You've outlived your usefulness to me anyway. Iron Aerospace is no place for bleeding hearts."

A bang rattled the hangar, the noise echoing against the metal siding next to them. Hayley clapped her hands over her ears and screamed as Ward dropped to the earth with a thud. Red liquid streamed out from behind his back.

Their time had run out. They were going to die.

"At least he still had a heart," Natasha said. "He might have been a lackey for your horrific schemes, but even Ward understood that you've gone too far. Innocent lives aren't worth it, Jennifer. None of this is worth it. What is the point if you gain the whole world but lose your soul?"

"Soul? What are those going for these days? Oh, that's right. Nothing, because there is no value in morality. All it does is ensure that you're the last one on the playing field, the last person to get invited, the last one to get picked. And I'm not a 'last' kind of woman. I want to be number one."

"Second place isn't good enough?" Chris scoffed. "Being the most respected private technology corporation isn't enough for you?"

"Second place is the first loser, Agent Barton. So, no. I don't want qualifiers before my company's name, like 'private corporation.' I want to be the best, period."

Natasha coughed out a laugh. "You're far from that, because you never will be. Not like this."

Irons sighed and tapped the barrel of her gun against the side of her head. "None of you are going to cooperate—are you?" It wasn't a question that required a response. "I've tried. I really have. But since none of you can be trusted, I can't risk leaving any loose ends."

Beside him, Natasha sniffed. Chris sidled his eyes toward her, catching a glimpse so brief that it could have been mistaken for a nervous tic—but it had been enough to see the nod, the urgency in her eyes. In his peripheral vision, he caught sight of the splayed fingers on her left hand. She tucked in her thumb. Then her pinkie finger. Then her ring finger.

Irons sighed again. "I suppose I'll manage this some other way. Sorry, darling, but your time's up." Irons lowered the gun, leveling it at Hayley. Then she cocked her head, looked down at her clothes and smirked. "But I also like this suit."

Natasha tucked in her index finger, forming a closed fist, and everything seemed to happen at once.

Irons shoved Hayley forward as she squeezed

the trigger, and the satellite behind them exploded with an earth-shaking boom.

Natasha lunged at Irons as Chris knocked Hayley out of the path of Irons's bullet, taking everyone to the ground at the outside wall of the hangar as flames and debris rocketed through the air beside them. The hangar's metal siding protected them from the shrapnel, but there was no escaping the shock wave from the blast. Natasha covered her head with her hands, peering through just in time to kick Irons's gun across the ground and out of reach before the darkness took her.

When she came to, sirens blared in the distance. A flare of terror surged through her at the possibility that she might have lost all her memories for a second time, but the very fact that she remembered losing them at all had to be a sign that she was all right—but what about everyone else?

Adrenaline coursed through her veins, and her eyes snapped open. The air in the hangar was thick and hazy, but they'd all been thrown at least ten feet from the hangar door. Flames licked the edges of the blackened satellite, or at least what remained of it. Millions of dollars' worth of technology, gone in a split second.

And yet the sound of emergency services' sirens meant she'd made the right call. Now all they had to do was keep Irons subdued until the service vehicles arrived, so Natasha needed to grab Chris and Hayley, and—

She rolled onto her side and almost screamed in pain. She'd forgotten about the bullet wound on her side, because everything else hurt from being thrown in the explosion. She turned her head instead to see Chris wrapped around his daughter's body. Hayley looked so small and fragile in his arms. Neither of them moved.

Her heart caught in her throat.

And then Jennifer Irons took a shuddering breath and pushed up to a seated position, clutching her head with one hand. Blood seeped through her fingers and ran down the side of her face, but she merely blinked it away with a scowl and scanned the area. Then her eyes landed on the ruined satellite.

Irons screamed in anger, deep and primal, and Natasha's insides clenched so tightly she thought she might throw up. Had they not stopped Irons after all? After everything, would help be only minutes too late? Natasha spotted Irons's gun about five feet away. If Irons saw it first and reached it before emergency services got through the complex to them, would Irons simply shoot them out of anger, regardless of the consequences?

"What did you do?" Natasha knew the moment Irons saw it. The woman lunged toward the gun, crawling across the debris-laden asphalt to grasp at the weapon. At the same moment, a twitch of movement next to Chris caught the farthest edge of Natasha's peripheral vision. "You're going to pay for this—"

Suddenly, Irons's body stiffened, jerked, and she toppled sideways onto the ground. A light buzzing noise stopped as quickly as it had started—and several feet away, a sigh of relief cut through Natasha's utter shock.

Hayley held a Taser, pointed at Irons. She dropped it, used and spent, and laid her head back down on the earth.

Before Natasha could say a word, vehicles came screaming around the nearest corner of the building. Fire trucks, an ambulance, two police cars and a news van screeched to a halt beside the hangar bay. Vehicle doors opened and slammed shut as uniformed personnel jumped out and ran to assist them or scrambled to extinguish the burning satellite.

As Natasha blinked at the people who hurried toward them, she saw a shiny new Cadillac Escalade pull up beside the other vehicles. The Escalade looked…familiar. Hadn't her father always driven an Escalade? This one looked like it had come right off the lot. It had to be a coincidence. Why would her father be here?

"Hayley, are you all right?" She called to her daughter as paramedics knelt next to her, Hayley, Chris and Irons.

"I'll be okay, Mom" came her daughter's small voice.

Relief washed over her, but it was a short-lived victory. They hadn't yet heard from Chris. "Chris? Agent Barton?"

Silence. Then "I'll poke him" from Hayley, though the closest paramedic immediately scolded Hayley to be careful in case he had a spinal injury. "Mom, he's breathing."

"So I am," Chris mumbled. "Listen to the paramedics, kid. Let them check us over before we move. The blast threw us pretty hard."

Thank You, Lord. Natasha couldn't suppress the smile that sprang to her lips. Not even a father for a day, and he was already acting like one.

It took several minutes for the paramedics to check all their vitals and give them the go-ahead to stand up. Natasha's head spun, but she felt surprisingly clearheaded despite all that had happened. As Chris spoke to the police, Hayley ran over and gave her a hug, which Natasha readily returned. Moments later, they watched Irons get loaded onto a stretcher, handcuffed to the gurney and rolled into an ambulance. It zoomed off with a police car following close behind. Natasha imagined that an FBI escort would meet them soon.

"How are you feeling?" She brushed her daughter's hair out of her eyes and sensed Chris coming toward them. "It's okay to not be okay."

Hayley nodded, biting her lip. "She's going to jail, right? She can't come after us?"

"She most definitely is going to jail, and for a very long time." Chris sighed. "Thanks to you, actually. Where did you get that Taser?"

Hayley shrugged with a small grin. "When you knocked me out of the way, I saw it had fallen out of that other guy's pocket when he got...you know. It was right there when we fell to the ground, so I just grabbed it."

"Wow. Talk about quick thinking! Brave and resourceful. You'd make a great FBI agent." Chris grinned back at her, and Natasha's heart squeezed again. They had the same smile.

How had she gone for twelve years without knowing that he hadn't left them on purpose? How could her father have crafted such a deep, insidious lie, and worse, how could she have believed it? If their relationship hadn't been strained before, well, she had a thing or two to say to him now—

"I imagine we have quite a few things to talk about."

Natasha's entire body shuddered with shock. Had she imagined the sound of her father's voice? But no—she yanked her eyes away from her daughter and Chris to see her father standing fifteen feet away, as though her anger toward him had caused him to manifest directly in front of her.

"I guess that's your Escalade," she blurted. She didn't know whether to scream, to cry, to lash out or to simply turn her back on him. "An expensive squander so that you have the right look for the masses, as usual."

But her words turned to ash in her mouth as she met her father's gaze. Sadness and regret poured out of him, and instead of looking like the imposing, proud figure of her youth, he more resembled a wearied old man. Lines pulled at the sides of his face, and he clasped his hands together as though unsure what to do with them.

"Natasha, my precious daughter," he said, his voice wavering on each syllable. "I'm sorry."

SIXTEEN

Natasha felt like screaming. Why did he get to be sorry? He didn't get to just waltz into her life again and apologize and expect everything to be all right. Not after everything she'd learned today. "What are you even doing here? How did you know where to find me?"

Chris placed his hand on her arm, holding her back. His touch soothed the heat of her anger just enough to allow her to listen and process Chris's words. "It's my fault, Natasha. I called him and asked for help."

She stared at each of them in disbelief. *Chris* had asked for her father's help? "But why would you do that?"

"I had no other course of action left. I needed to find you as fast as possible, and I needed to get to you before the FBI placed you under arrest. Speaking of which—" He grimaced as a pair of FBI agents pulled into the facility and exited their vehicle, heading directly for Natasha.

Natasha's heart began to beat faster again. "Do they really have evidence against me? I thought Irons was bluffing."

"They found residue on your clothing, and the bullet that killed Cobie May matched the gun that was next to you when you woke up on the highway." He addressed the FBI agents who hesitated, seeing Chris protectively grip her shoulder. "Hold on, boys. I witnessed a direct confession to the murders of three national assets by Brett Ward and Jennifer Irons. I suggest you subpoena the security tapes from this facility immediately, but get someone in there right away to make sure they're not destroyed. You'll find all the evidence needed for prosecution on those tapes."

The FBI agents took off. Next to Natasha, a paramedic attempted to get a word in edgewise about getting her and Chris both to the hospital to take care of their gunshot wounds.

"I'm not going anywhere until I get some answers about my father," she said, leaning into Chris for support. One of the paramedics had given her a painkiller to numb the injury, but it appeared to be wearing off—or maybe all the other injuries were simply wearing through. "Why did you come here? You hate Chris and you always have, and you've never been supportive of my decision to become an astronaut with NASA."

The man's eyes filled with tears, and the stone wall around Natasha's heart began to crack.

"I've been so wrong, Natasha. Please forgive me."

She couldn't. She just couldn't.

"When Agent Barton phoned to tell me that you and Hayley were in danger… I suppose it was the first time that I truly realized I might lose you both. Forever. And when he asked me to help, it occurred to me that even if I could help…you might not want me to. We've spent the entirety of our adult lives apart, and it's my fault. I was too proud, too self-absorbed to see beyond the end of my nose, and hearing Barton brought the realization that I've done the very same thing to Hayley. My attitude, how I treated you, caused you to spend twelve years without a father in your life, and she's never known hers. I imagine your mother would have a thing or two to say to me about this if she were alive today, and I'd be ashamed for her to see what's become of us. I don't want to be the reason my granddaughter feels the same way about her own father as you do about me."

"You did that, Dad. You convinced me to doubt him. You told me that he'd use my baby for leverage against the family. I believe your words were to 'disengage with those degenerates before they attempt to drag our name through the mud by association.' And I was too young to understand what you were doing. I was pregnant and scared, and you made me believe that the man I loved didn't want me anymore because of it. Your lies made me question his motives for loving me. I accept blame for believing you, I won't deny my free will and the choices I made, but I've known for a long time that the way you view and treat people different from you is wrong."

"I know." Senator Stark's voice cracked. "I *was* wrong. I thought only of myself and my political career, not of my innocent daughter caught up on the tumultuous waters of life. I shouldn't have regarded you as a vessel of family shame. I was caught up in my prejudiced beliefs and I passed them on to you, causing my granddaughter to grow up fatherless because of my selfish ambition. I don't know how to make it up to you, and I don't know if I ever will, but I do know that I'll support your work at NASA however I can from this day forward. I'll push for more funding. I'll propose social awareness programs."

"You don't have to do that, Dad." Natasha felt the tears well in her own eyes. "I know how you feel about space travel programs and government funding for scientific research."

"I've been a crusty old dog, daughter. I allowed myself to be purposefully misinformed and blinded, and I passed my damaging beliefs on to you. I'm so proud that you've overcome it—you went your own way and you've done amazing things. I know you'll do many more. I'm so sorry." He buried his face in his hands, and Natasha felt frozen to the spot. What should she do?

Chris reacted before she did. Her breath caught in her throat as he slipped from her side and crossed the pavement. Of all the people standing there, she'd expected him to be the last person to reach out and grasp her father's shoulder. Her father dropped his hands and stared at Chris in surprise. Then, in the last gesture she ever expected to see, Chris drew her father into a hug.

Natasha was overcome and unable to hold back, and the tears spilled from her eyes with such force that she barely heard the small, awe-filled voice of the girl standing next to her.

"Uh, Mom? Did Grandpa just say that Agent Barton is my father?"

Chris supervised the transfer of Ward into another ambulance, ensuring that he too was handcuffed and strapped in. The emergency response paramedics were unsure as to whether the man would make it—Irons's shot might have punctured a lung and Ward had lost a lot of blood, but his body was fighting hard to pull through. Chris hoped he survived long enough to expose the rest of the truth about Irons's schemes, and for justice to be served. No matter a person's crimes, additional loss of life was never the desired ending.

After convening with the other FBI agents and local law enforcement on the scene regarding the next steps to take, he crossed the pavement to Natasha's father again. The senator stood by his Escalade, looking like he wanted to help but unsure if his presence was even welcome.

Chris extended his hand to the man. "Sir, thank you again. It's probably best if you take off, however. Natasha is going to need some time to process everything—these events, you being here. *Me* being here. She'll come to you in time, but I'd recommend giving her some space to come to terms with your apology—and with the truth."

Senator Stark nodded and shook Chris's hand, one firm pump. "Of course. I would expect no less. And thank you for your forgiveness, however undeserved."

Chris smiled and glanced back at Natasha, who was currently fighting with a paramedic over whether NASA policy required her to travel in an ambulance back to the hospital. "That's the thing about forgiveness, sir. No one deserves it."

The senator sniffed and tapped the car door. "Wise words, son." Chris startled, uncertain whether he'd heard the man right. But Natasha's father smiled and began to back into the passenger seat of the Escalade. "Have a merry Christmas. And save me a seat at the wedding, will you?"

He shut the car door and the vehicle pulled away, leaving Chris standing in shock—and with a tinge of warm satisfaction at the man's insinuation. *Wise words, sir.*

"Hayley!" Natasha's voice echoed across the open space. "Come here, please!"

But then he felt a tug on his sleeve. Hayley materialized by his side, her expression serious and filled with concern. "Agent Barton?"

My daughter. Nerves immediately flared in his stomach. "Yes?"

She crossed her arms and raised an eyebrow at him. "Are you actually my father?"

How did he respond to that with anything but the truth? He looked across the asphalt at Natasha, who'd frozen in place, her complexion pale as she waited for his response, knowing what her daughter had asked. Did she not think he'd tell Hayley the truth? Or was she afraid that he would?

Did she think that he didn't care?

"Yes," he said, choosing his words carefully. He'd faced down death countless times over the past few days, feared for his life and Natasha's life, and yet he'd never felt more nervous than in this very moment. "And I'm so sorry that I haven't been there for you all these years. I honestly didn't even know that you existed, which sounds awful…but it's the truth. You can ask your mother if you want to know more, but please understand, now that I've found you, I will *never* abandon you. I'd love to get to know you, to be a part of your life, if you'll let me. If your mother will let me."

Hayley smirked and shrugged. "*Okaaaay*... I guess. It's kind of cool to have an FBI agent for a dad."

"I'm glad you think so."

"Do you still love her?"

Chris blinked at Hayley, stunned by the question. "Do I…love her? Your mother?"

"Yeah. If you're going to be a part of my life, I don't want it if it's going to make her upset or if you're going to resent her being around, too."

He glanced at Natasha, who pressed her lips together as they locked eyes. He thought about everything they'd been through, from the first time they'd met as teenagers until this moment, and all the times she'd come to mind ever since—despite his attempts to push her out of his memories, even requesting to begin his FBI career on the other side of the country just so that he wouldn't run into her by accident.

And then he'd been transferred here, accepted a missing person's case and come face-to-face with her, like it was meant to be. As though God had a plan for them all along.

As though they'd needed to learn and grow and mature as individuals first.

I guess You really do care, God. The realization was just as surprising as the remaining force of his love for Natasha, even after twelve years apart.

He held her gaze as he spoke. “Yes. I do.”

Natasha’s lips parted in a soft gasp, and he crossed the space to reach her in the span of a heartbeat. He took her into his arms and held her close, gentle and aware of her injury. She really did need to get to a hospital—it was unbelievable that she’d remained standing for so long. But wasn’t that what she’d trained for, what had defined her all these years? Prepared for anything, ready to face life-and-death scenarios head-on, this time literally, and still keep going. He was glad for it, because it meant he could hold her like this. She fit in his arms the way she always had, like the twelve years apart had only been twelve minutes.

He tilted his head to whisper in her ear. “I still love you.” This time, the declaration was for her and her alone. “I always have.”

Natasha’s breath hitched as she buried her face in his chest. “I love you, too, Chris Barton. It’d be a lot easier if I didn’t, but I do.”

An idea burst into his head, unfurling like

a tulip in the morning sunlight. "So…do you want to pick up where we left off?"

Natasha pulled back and looked at him inquisitively. "Where we left off?"

He nodded. "I don't want to waste any more time before spending the rest of my life with you, the way I'd planned to twelve years ago. My intentions and my feelings toward you haven't changed."

"Chris…what are you saying?"

Behind them, Hayley squealed, figuring out Chris's meaning before Natasha did. With his heart hammering a hole through his sternum, Chris drew away from Natasha and knelt, holding fast to both her hands. He placed a tender kiss on each wrist, then clasped his palms over hers.

Then he spoke the words that he'd already heard an answer to, twelve years ago—and that he prayed he'd receive the same answer to today. "Natasha Stark, will you give me the best Christmas gift a man could ever receive… and marry me?"

Her laugh and beaming smile, plus a cheer from Hayley, told him the answer before she even spoke the words. "Of course I will, Christopher Barton. And this time my answer is final. No one and nothing will change that."

He didn't wait another second to draw her close and kiss her again.

EPILOGUE

Ten days later...

Natasha cupped Chris's cheek as he moved toward her as if in slow motion. The little smirk on his face told her that he was enjoying this, taking his time while all eyes were on them both. He paused, his lips hovering but a breath above hers, before she gave in to impatience and pressed a kiss to his lips.

The assembled outdoor audience roared with delight, sending up cheers and whoops. There was a sudden, furious clicking of camera shutters closing and opening, as well as a flurry of cell phone camera blips as the operators snapped with abandon.

She loved his mischievous side, and she loved that he hadn't changed a single bit in their years apart. Well, maybe a bit. They both had, but for the better. Without that change, that shift in perspective, neither of them would be here.

Chris drew her back upright when the pastor cleared his throat, and released her once she found solid footing again. She felt her face flush as Chris drew away and they both opened their eyes, heat rushing to her neck and cheeks. Chris winked, the very picture of a man hopelessly in love and wanting the rest of the world to know it.

And he was in love with *her*. Still. After everything.

In less than two weeks, he'd become the perfect father to Hayley, trying to make up for lost time without pressuring the girl to accept him before she was ready. Natasha hadn't previously told her daughter much about her father and Hayley hadn't asked, and it had been good to sit down together and tell the whole tale from start to finish. And afterward, it had been Hayley who'd invited Chris to come to their place for Christmas breakfast and to open gifts together like a family. Two days ago, Chris and Hayley had gone on a father-daughter outing by themselves for the very first time, and they'd both come back with many stories to tell and a few inside jokes they'd decided to keep secret from Natasha.

She didn't mind, not one bit. Certainly there'd be tough times ahead—she didn't relish the first time they'd have to discipline Hayley together, or dealing with her teenage years, of which on some days the mouthing off and rebellion already seemed to have begun—but the pure truth was that she and Chris would face it together. As equals. They had each other for support and reliance, and the three of them would build this little family back up in strength and faith.

Chris must have felt her gaze lingering on him, because he leaned over for one final quick peck on the lips, interrupting the pastor's efforts to introduce the couple. He broke away with a sheepish grin and a quiet "Sorry!" to the pastor, then took Natasha's hand and faced the assembled crowd of family, friends and coworkers.

"Ladies and gentlemen, please rise," the pastor said, his voice booming throughout the Rocket Garden courtyard of the Kennedy Space Center Visitor Complex. "Now presenting the happy couple."

Chris raised their hands in a victory pump, then leaned over and gently kissed her cheek.

What a blessing that the venue had availability during the holiday season so they could get married so soon after finding each other again. What a blessing that the sun shone brightly today. It truly was the perfect Christmas gift.

And what an even greater blessing that her father stood quietly in the last row of seats, eyes beaming with pride—even though his expression reflected an uncertainty as to whether he was wanted there at all. Natasha paused, pulling Chris to a stop. He nodded at her and released her hand so she could give her father the first hug they'd shared in over a decade.

"I'm so glad you came," she said, realizing she truly meant it.

"I told Chris to save me a seat," he replied. "Of course I came. Congratulations. You look so beautiful. I'm so proud of the woman you've become."

And with that, she took Chris's hand once more, smiling at the sight of her gold name bracelet around her wrist, a reminder that her heart had always been his—even when she hadn't been willing to admit it to herself. Their romance certainly hadn't been all butterflies and blushes, but she'd take bullets and Christmas bells any day, so long as they had each other.

With their daughter following behind as maid of honor, the trio stepped forward, beyond the crowd and into the future, together.

* * * * *

If you enjoyed SILENT NIGHT THREAT,
look for these other books by Michelle Karl
from Love Inspired Suspense:

FATAL FREEZE
UNKNOWN ENEMY
OUTSIDE THE LAW

Dear Reader,

Thank you so much for spending a little slice of your holidays with Chris and Natasha! You're probably wondering about the Orion space program that features in this story—is the race to Mars a real thing? Sure is! NASA's Orion program is real, and it's under way, though I accelerated the timeline here for the sake of story. But you can read all about it on NASA's website and elsewhere online.

Those of you who've read *Outside the Law* will likely recognize Natasha's last name. She's the niece of a dastardly character from that book, but she has worked hard to make a name for herself in a typically male-dominated field. I believe that as long as we're following God's leading in our lives, we can accomplish great things. Sometimes it will require leaning on a trusted team for support. Sometimes it will mean sacrifice. But when we're inside God's will, our lives are forever changed.

I love hearing from readers. Find me on Twitter (@_MichelleKarl_) or at michellekarl.com and let me know if you're having a snowy or sunny Christmas. Have a merry Christmas and happy New Year, friends!

Blessings,
Michelle